A PAST FORGIVEN (CONTEMPORARY CHRISTIAN NEW ADULT ROMANCE)

A HEARTBEATS UNIVERSITY ROMANCE

LORANA HOOPES

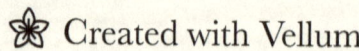 Created with Vellum

DEDICATION

Dedication Page:

To my family who allows me to sacrifice time with them to write these stories.

To my friends who inspire me even when you don't know it.

To women everywhere who have been forced to do things against your will, your Heavenly Father loves you.

NOTE FROM THE AUTHOR

Thank you so much for picking up this book. I hope you enjoy the story and the characters as they are dear to my heart. If you do, please leave a review at your retailer. It really does make a difference because it lets people make an informed decision about books. Below are the other books in this series. I would love for you to check them out. I'd also like to offer you a sample of my newest book. Free Sample!

Sign up for Lorana Hoopes's newsletter and get her book, The Billionaire's Impromptu Bet, as a welcome gift. Get Started Now!

The Heartbeats series:

The Power of Prayer

Where It All Began

When Hearts Collide

CHAPTER 1

*J*ess Peterson stepped off the bus onto the campus of Texas Tech and took a deep breath. Though not her first choice of colleges - she'd wanted to get farther away - at least it removed her from the clutches of her "handsy" stepfather. In fact, if she never saw Paducah, Texas and it's one stoplight again, she would be fine with that.

She slung her black backpack over her shoulder and crossed the quad to Knapp Hall. A folded map resided in the back pocket of her cutoff denim shorts. However, Jess possessed a photographic memory and had memorized most of the buildings, on the east side of campus at least. Knapp Hall was a large, though non-descript, brick building of three floors built in 1948.

Jess registered the cracks in the cement steps as she pulled open the front door. They weren't surprising as old as the building was, but she hoped the interior had been updated more recently.

It was not to be. The dorm had been improved since 1948, but it still looked to be about ten years behind the times in terms of decorating. Variations of browns and greens were the main colors, interspersed with a few streaks of gray.

After stopping at the information desk on the first floor just long enough to get the keys, Jess took the stairs at the end of the hall two at a time to the third floor.

316. The closed door elicited a glimmer of hope that they'd gotten her the single she'd requested. She did not want a roommate.

As the door swung open, Jess swore softly under her breath. A blonde girl stood beside the left bed unpacking the suitcase in front of her. She looked up when Jess entered and smiled. Jess did not return the smile as she asked, "Who are you?"

The girl dropped the item of clothing she had been holding and stepped forward, extending her hand. "I'm Emily. I guess you're my new roommate."

Rolling her eyes, Jess pushed past the girl, ignoring the hand. "Crap. I told them I needed a single."

"Well, they ran out," Emily stated, appearing unperturbed by the rude behavior. "See, I'm a sophomore, but I offered to room with an incoming freshman if it was necessary. Since you're here," she shrugged, "I guess it was necessary."

Jess tossed her backpack on the right bed and glared at the blonde. "Well, I'll be telling them to look again. I don't do roommates." Her hand plunged into the backpack, rifling through the contents until she found the item she was looking for - the paperwork with the RA's name on it. Ah, there it was. Clasping it in her hand, she glared at Emily again, and then abruptly left the room, slamming the wooden door behind her. "Nope, nu uh," she muttered as she stomped down the hallway to the RA's room.

Room 350 was at the far end of the hall, and Jess rapped loudly on the wooden door when she arrived. A tall, leggy blonde with sparkly pink lips opened the door. "Hi, can I help you?"

Oh, great. My RA was probably the prom

queen - every year, Jess thought as she shoved the paper clenched in her fist in front of the preppy blonde's face. "I'm Jess Peterson, and I'm supposed to have a single, but there's some goody-two-shoes who has already unpacked her things in my room."

The RA's perfectly arched eyebrows shot to the top of her forehead as she leaned back slightly and took the paper, lowering it to a level she could read it from. "Okay, well, first off, let's try not to call our roommate names." She unfolded the paper and glanced over it.

With crossed arms, Jess tapped her foot against the carpeted floor as she waited for the RA to explain they had made a mistake.

The RA looked up from the paper and sighed. "This says we'd try to get you a single, but that we couldn't guarantee it. Apparently, more upperclassmen returned than expected, and they get their choice of a single first. So, I can add you to the waiting list, but I'm afraid you're stuck for now."

Heat erupted in Jess's body and her hands clenched into fists at her side. "That's it? That's all you can do?"

The blonde shrugged and held the paper out to her. "Maybe try to get to know your roommate. I bet she's not as bad as you think."

"Aargh, you are worthless." Jess snatched the paper back from the RA's glittery pink nails and marched down the stairs. This could NOT be happening. She slammed the outside door open as she reached the final step. It banged against the wall before slamming shut, satisfying a small destructive desire burning within.

Leaning against the brick wall, she pulled a cigarette and a lighter out of the pocket of her shorts and flicked the lighter on. As she puffed on the cigarette, the nicotine went to work on her nerves, soothing some of the manic feeling. How was she going to make it through a semester with a roommate?

It wasn't that she'd never lived with anyone. She'd crashed with a few friends the last few months after moving out of her mom's house, but that had been a necessary evil and she'd been hoping to finally have a place of her own when she arrived at college.

As she inhaled, plans formulated in her mind. Maybe if living with her was awful enough, she could get the girl to leave. What would it take? Loud music? Being a slob? A parade of men? She would have to try them all until one worked.

The cigarette burned to a nub, and Jess dropped it to the ground, squishing it into the dirt with the toe of her boot before deciding to take a walk to calm her anger and solidify a plan.

When she returned to the room later, the girl was still there and had decorated. Red and black towels, displaying Tech pride, hung from the handle by the sink. Pictures of the Eiffel tower covered the wall above a soft grey bedspread etched with a black Flëur De Leis. The girl sat on the bed with a book open on her lap. Ice flooded Jess's veins as she realized what the girl was reading. She hadn't thought this roommate situation could get worse, but she'd been wrong.

"Oh heck no, you're one of those?"

"I'm sorry, one of what?" The girl's brow wrinkled as she looked at Jess.

"One of those Bible beaters." Jess had known enough "religious" people in her lifetime to know she wanted nothing to do with them. They always talked a big talk, but they never lived what they preached.

Even her mother attended a church for a time, but dropped it when she met Jim.

The girl smiled. "I am a Christ follower, if that's what you mean."

With another eye roll, Jess mumbled under her breath, "Great, they paired me with a religious nut job." She grabbed her headphones from her bag, plugged them into her phone, and turned up the music. Though the girl said nothing, Jess could tell the music was bugging her, and she smiled a little inside. Maybe this wouldn't be too hard after all.

A few minutes later, the girl motioned for Jess to remove the headphones. She pushed one back just enough to hear the girl ask something about food. *Yeah, as if I'd want to eat with you.* Jess flicked a hand at her in dismissal and sighed in relief when the door closed behind the girl.

Turning off the music, she began to unpack her own things. There wasn't much, only what would fit in her large backpack. When she'd left home a few months back, she had taken only a few clothes and items, just enough to get by. She'd stayed with a few acquaintances through the summer before having to spend the last week in a shelter. It hadn't been that bad, and it allowed her to keep the small wad of money she managed to save up and keep hidden from her mother.

Thankfully, a scholarship arrived her senior year that covered college room and board. No fan of high school, Jess had done as little to get by as possible. But her Junior year, the guidance counselor, who understood a little of her unfortunate home situation, convinced Jess she was a good student and could get a scholarship if she worked hard. The counselor had been right, and the scholarship had been Jess's ticket out of the abuse she'd lived with for the last several years.

Jess pulled out her favorite black blanket, unrolled it, and covered the bed. As she looked at the bare walls, she wished she could have brought some posters from home, but there'd been no room. Her small wardrobe filled most of the space in the backpack along with necessary items. The contrast between her blank, monochromatic side of the room and the other girl's pride-filled side was nauseating and slightly comical.

An audible rumbling in her stomach sounded, and Jess realized she was hungry after all, but she had no idea which dorm the blonde saint had gone to. Knapp Hall didn't have a full cafeteria, but many of the nearby dorms did. As she didn't want to risk running into her, Jess decided it was time to see what the town offered.

University Avenue lay to the east, and

she trekked that direction having seen a few restaurants from the bus when she arrived earlier. The sun still shone, though it was nearing dusk, and beads of sweat trickled down one side of her neck. She had shaved the other side hoping to deter her stepfather's advances, but it hadn't worked. However, it seemed to fit well with her "don't mess with me" attitude, so she'd kept it.

She crossed University at a crosswalk and debated. A pizza place, a burger joint, and a pancake house dotted the row of buildings. Not feeling much like breakfast or a greasy pizza, Jess opted for the burger joint, Ollie's.

The red and black building oozed Tech pride, and a picture of Ollie, a white dog with a black patch over one eye and a red bandana, completed the sign. Jess sighed at the gimmicky exterior, but figured the food couldn't be too bad. It was rather hard to mess up a burger and fries.

As she opened the door, second thoughts flooded her mind. She might as well have walked into an updated version of Cheers. Huge television screens adorned the walls. Booths covered in red vinyl hugged the large windows, and a few tables and chairs crowded a large bar. A lively group filled the room, including a group of jocks at the nearest table cheering at the big screens. Pretty, blonde girls in designer clothes sat at another table tapping away on their expensive cell phones. If there were two things Jess couldn't stand, it was jocks and Barbies.

She paused, hand on the door, and debated her options. Though not her scene, she was hungry, and there were a few empty booths. The renewed rumbling of her stomach finalized the decision, and with a clenched jaw, she crossed to a nearby empty booth. Why couldn't she be old enough to sit at the bar and order a stiff tequila drink?

She'd been drinking since the age of fourteen when she'd found the liquor in her mother's stash. The first swig had been awful, but she'd found after that the lightheaded sensation helped her forget the leers and touches of her stepfather. Jess wouldn't say she had acquired a taste for the liquor, but she had developed an appreciation to the mindless bliss it offered.

A college-aged waiter, clad in a white t-shirt, shorts, and bored expression arrived shortly and handed her a menu. New fears of the quality of the food deepened as the sticky menu ripped open with a squelching sound. Swallowing her disgust, Jess ordered a burger, fries, and a diet coke.

As the waiter turned away and headed

to the kitchen, a large male slid in the booth across from her. With his short brown hair and broad shoulders, he looked very much like all the other jocks at the nearby table. A quick glance that direction confirmed her suspicion as the whole table had their eyes glued Jess's direction. The guy wasn't bad looking, but Jess held no love for jocks. Perhaps if she could give him a cold enough stare he would leave, but alas he opened his mouth, and at the sound of his thick southern drawl, Jess felt IQ points trickle out of her head.

"I haven't seen you 'round here before," the behemoth said. "I'm Randy. I'm a linebacker."

Though Jess watched football - she was, in fact, a closet Dallas Cowboys fan - she had no intention of letting this dolt know it.

"That's nice," she said sweetly,

plastering a fake smile on her face, "now get out of my booth." The last words dripped with venom as her smile dropped and she glared daggers at him.

Randy held up his hands in defense. "Whoa, no need to be rude now. I just thought I'd say hi."

"Hi, now please leave."

"Whatever." He unfolded himself from the booth and lumbered back to his friends who cheered and clapped.

Jess rolled her eyes and sighed. Maybe she should have ordered in. She turned her attention out the window, and as she watched the cars pass, she wished for a different life. Thankfully, the table of jocks decided she wasn't worth any more trouble and left her alone.

A few moments later, her plate of greasy food arrived. Jess hadn't thought a restaurant could mess up a burger and fries, but she had been wrong. There was so much sauce on the burger that the bun had begun to disintegrate, and she was forced to eat the patty with a fork. The fries had evidently sat in the fryer a little too long as they were no longer a golden yellow, but an odd rusty brownish color. She could make a scene—demand a refund—but she wanted no more attention tonight. Better to just let it be and mark this as a place to never revisit. She shoveled down what little she could to satisfy the rumbling, paid the tab, and left. It was still better than home, she reminded herself as she stepped out into the humid night.

"Hey, you got a light?"

The voice came from the right where a guy with dark hair and a black leather jacket stood. Stubble covered his chin, making his blue eyes shine like a beacon in a dark storm, and the hint of a tattoo peeked over his collar. Jess's breath caught as her heart hammered in her chest. He reminded her of Adrian Paul's Highlander, a show that had originally aired before her time but that she had fallen in love with when re-runs began.

She nodded, forcing her voice to stay cool as she reached for her lighter. A slight tremor gripped her hand as she held it out, but he didn't seem to notice. He lit his cigarette and then handed the lighter back. Jess shook out her own cigarette and lit up next to him.

"What's your name?" he asked, nodding at her and taking a deep breath of smoke. It curled out of his thin lips in little wisps. Jess had never wanted to be a cigarette so badly.

"Jess. You?" She breathed in a deep lungful, careful not to overdo it. A coughing fit in front of this Adonis would be mortifying.

"Chad. You go to Tech?"

"Yeah, I just got here."

He nodded again and continued puffing. Jess watched as his hand rose to his mouth and lowered to his side in a rhythmic motion, and she wondered what the stubble on his face would feel like against her cheek. Would it be rough like sandpaper or was it softer? A heat seared across her face, and she turned away.

"Well, I guess I'll see you around." He finished his cigarette, flicked it on the ground, and then mounted a black Harley Davidson parked at the curb. His bad boy quotient rose even higher, and her heart pounded faster as she envisioned herself climbing on the back and wrapping her arms around his waist, the smell of his leather jacket tickling her nose.

As the engine roared to life, the image vanished, and the pounding in her heart slowed. He flicked a mock salute and rode away. Sighing, Jess finished her cigarette and began the trek back to the dorm room.

When the building came into view, her good mood faded away. If only she didn't have the perky roommate to put up with.

With a sigh, she pushed open the door to the shared room. Emily looked up from her book, but said nothing. Crossing to the little sink, Jess brushed her teeth, changed into her sleeping attire of a long t-shirt, and then flicked off the overhead light.

"Excuse me, but I was reading." Emily's voice held a note of annoyance, and Jess smiled to herself in the darkness.

"And now you're not," she retorted.

A sigh carried across the room, followed by the sound of rummaging around in a drawer. There was a click, and a little book light came on. Jess should have known Emily would be a prepared little Girl Scout. She rolled her eyes and turned to face the wall. Score one for the annoying blonde, but there was always tomorrow. She would just have to be more creative.

~

*A*s Chad turned off the motorcycle and dismounted, his mind revisited the raven-haired girl. With one side or her hair shaved and a nose ring, she was definitely trying to portray a tough exterior, but though he hadn't spoken with her long, he had sensed a sadness in her eyes. It was the same sadness he often saw reflected in his mirror, and he wondered what hurt resided in her past.

He hadn't always been into analyzing people. When he'd first come to Texas Tech, it had been to major in Mechanical

Engineering, but two years ago his younger brother had been killed in a school shooting and everything had changed. Chad had turned from mechanical engineering to psychology, desperate for answers as to why people acted the way they did. He still wasn't sure what he planned to do with the degree, but if he could save even one person from going through the fate Kyle had or dealing with the aftermath as he was having to, it would be worth it.

He flicked on the light of his small apartment-like dorm room and sighed. The benefit of being a Junior was that he could live in West Village, but as he'd opted for a single apartment this year, the downfall was that loneliness often crept in.

Chad thought about calling one of his "hook-ups," but it would be his first day teaching tomorrow. His time would be better spent making sure he was prepared as he needed to keep this job to afford his housing. Besides, he was rather tired of last year's offerings. Hopefully, this year would wield some new and exciting flavors.

Again the girl from earlier flashed into his mind. She had been attracted to him. He had seen it in her face before she turned away, and she might be interesting. At least interesting enough for some good times. It was too bad he hadn't gotten her number. Tech was a big campus and the chances he would see her again were small.

He pushed the thoughts of her from his mind and focused on arranging his papers and rehearsing his lecture. Tomorrow would be soon enough to focus on finding new women to add to his list.

CHAPTER 2

*J*ess woke to the sun streaming in the window. Yawning, she stretched and sneaked a glance at the other side of the room. Emily's bed was made, but she was nowhere to be seen. A smile played across Jess's face as she realized she had the room to herself, for a bit at least. Who knew when the blonde would be back.

Ugh, she hated school, not because she was bad at it, but because it bored her. The only good thing about college was the ability to take afternoon classes. Not being a morning person, Jess rarely functioned well before her first cup of coffee.

What did she have today? Closing her eyes, she pictured her schedule - just Psychology and Math. Neither were her favorite subject, but she had taken Psychology hoping she'd learn to analyze people. Math, on the other hand, was just one of those stupid required classes in college. She knew basic math, enough to balance a checkbook and pay bills. Since math didn't change, anything beyond that seemed useless.

Rolling out of bed, Jess padded to the little cloudy mirror. The non-shaved side of her hair looked like it had been in a windstorm. She yanked a brush through it, hoping to tame it a little, but the result wasn't much better. With a shrug, she picked up her toothbrush, and after brushing her teeth, she pulled on a pair of black shorts and a matching tank top. Then she grabbed her books and a granola bar and headed downstairs.

Though the dorm didn't have a full cafeteria, a coffee pot sat on the table by the main desk, so she stopped to fill up a Styrofoam cup. It was strong, but not awful, and it would do until she could get a better cup.

As she pushed open the main doors, Jess's skin prickled at the change in temperature. The dorm stayed at a constant temperature of seventy-two, cool but not cold. However, the blazing sun outside made Jess glad she opted for shorts. She took a left towards the Psychology building.

One of the blander buildings on campus, the Psychology building was a giant brick rectangle with a myriad of windows. Jess pushed open the door and turned left to find room 110. The wooden door opened to a large lecture hall filled with rows of seats—almost like a movie theater except each seat contained a pull-out desk top on the side and was made of hard plastic instead of the comfy foam you found in the theater.

Jess took a seat at the back. She hated having people behind her, analyzing her, criticizing her. A handful of other people sat in the back row, and a few heads dotted the closer rows, but the room was mostly empty. Turning her wrist, she checked her watch to see ten minutes still remained until the class started. For once, she was early.

The door continued to open and more people filed in, filling the room, but none of them looked like someone Jess wanted to talk to. Slouching down in the chair, she pulled out her phone and aimlessly flicked through social media posts. She wasn't sure why she still bothered as she had no one she kept in touch with, having burned all her old bridges when she left Paducah.

A few minutes later, the door down front opened, and a dark-haired man entered. He laid a satchel on the table, and when he looked up, Jess's breath caught in her throat. Chad, the handsome biker from the night before, stood down front. She sat up straighter in her seat and wished for once she'd sat in the front row. This had just gotten interesting.

"I'm Chad Michaels, and I'm your TA for this class. Dr. Warren will rarely be here, though you can catch him in his office during office hours. I'm passing around your syllabus. Read it, live it, love it. Hopefully you already purchased the required reading because you need to read the first five chapters before our next meeting."

Chad continued speaking as he handed a stack of papers to the first row, but all Jess focused on was the sweet melody of his voice. She'd been attracted to him before, but now that he was basically the instructor, her desire for him increased.

As class ended, she realized she couldn't recall a single thing he had said after his name. She would have to hope everything he'd said was in the syllabus. Pretending to gather her books, Jess waited until most of the students left before ambling down front.

"Well, I didn't know I'd be seeing you again so soon," she said, turning on her most seductive voice and tucking a strand of dark hair behind her ear.

He looked up and narrowed his eyes, obviously trying to place her face. Then they widened as recognition flashed in them and he nodded, "Ah, Lighter Girl. You have time to get a smoke now?"

Jess shrugged, feigning indifference. No need to let him know how attracted she was to him. Though she had math in twenty minutes, getting to know Chad seemed a little more important at the moment. She flashed what she hoped was a sexy smile, lowered her lids, and said, "Sure. Why not?"

He packed up his bag, and they headed out the side door. A shadow covered this side of the building, but it wasn't much cooler. They each pulled out a cigarette, and Jess produced her lighter.

"How long have you been a TA?" she asked him, trying to start up a conversation.

"It's my first year. You can't be a TA until your Junior year." He took a deep puff, and Jess forced her eyes away from his lips.

"Oh." *Stupid,* Jess thought, *stop asking stupid questions.*

"Where are you from?" he asked.

"A little Podunk town, Paducah. How about you?"

A tiny smile tugged at the corners of his mouth. "California originally, but when we moved out here, we lived in Seminole. It's a small town too." He finished his cigarette and then glanced at his watch. "I have to get to an appointment, but give me your phone."

The request took her off guard, but Jess pulled out her phone and handed it over. Chad's finger moved deftly over the screen. Then he flashed a sexy smile and handed the phone back. "I put my cell number in there. Text me so I have your number too."

Jess grasped the phone and bit the inside of her lip to keep from smiling like an idiot. "I'll do that."

He flicked a wave and sauntered off, and she strolled to math class on cloud nine. She'd only be a little late, and she doubted anyone would even notice.

When Jess returned to the dorm room that afternoon, Emily was gone. Jess sat on her bed, pulled out her phone, and flicked to Chad's number. She was looking forward to using it in the next few days. Not right away, but soon. Had to play at least a little hard to get. She laid the phone down and glanced over at Emily's side of the room. The Bible Emily had been reading the night before lay on her nightstand. Jess didn't know why, but the desire to look inside it suddenly burned within her.

After glancing at the door, she crossed to Emily's bed, sat down, and grabbed the book. It was heavier than she'd expected. The black, textured cover held Emily's name embossed in gold in the bottom right corner. Emily Peters. As Jess opened the cover, the words "To Emily, Love Mom and Dad" mocked her. Had she ever had a mom and dad who truly loved her? She held no memory of her biological father, but she had once believed her mother loved her, until the latest step-father entered the picture.

Jess flipped a few pages in and read the headings: Reward for Obedience, Punishment for Disobedience... Well, that didn't sound inspiring. A few more flips: The Lord Calls Samuel, The Philistines Capture the Ark. Who were the Philistines? She didn't remember them from History class. Another flip landed her in Psalms 106. "Praise the Lord. Give thanks to the Lord, for He is good; His love endures forever." Jess snorted. She had never felt any love from God if He was even real.

An exasperated sigh tumbled out of

her lips. Nothing amazing resided in there, just a bunch of history and nonsense. Exactly what she thought. She slammed the book shut, tossing it back on Emily's nightstand before heading out to grab food.

~

"Well, how was the first day," Dr. Warren asked as Chad entered the small office. Dr. Warren was nearing seventy with a full head of white hair and matching bushy eyebrows.

"It went pretty well," Chad said. "It's a large class." He didn't mention the fact he was attracted to one of the students. Even though a TA and not the actual professor, he was pretty sure a relationship would be frowned upon.

"I have no doubt in your ability," Dr. Warren said. "If I had, I wouldn't have asked you to TA for me." Dr. Warren's tenured status allowed him the option to have a TA teach one or two of his classes so he could focus on the students seeking a doctorate. He had asked Chad to take over the Intro to Psychology class at the end of the previous school year.

"Thank you, sir. I won't let you down," Chad said, "but I better be getting back to my room. I have a lot of work from business class this morning. I'll see you on Wednesday." Chad had put most of his classes on Tuesday and Thursday when he didn't have to teach, but his business classes were only offered on Mondays and Wednesdays so he'd had to schedule them before his teaching.

Dr. Warren absentmindedly waved a hand at Chad as he returned to whatever he had been working on when Chad walked in.

As he crossed the campus back to his

dorm, Chad's eyes took in the beautiful women in their crop tops and short shirts. Lubbock's warm weather and long summers often meant shorter shorts and tighter tops as women tried to escape the heat. Not that Chad minded the view, but today his mind kept returning to Jess. Maybe it was the look in her eyes, but something about her made him want to get to know her better.

~

*E*mily was in the room when Jess returned that evening. She glanced up from the book she was reading and asked, "How was your first day?"

Jess glared at her. Did the girl honestly think they were going to be friends? "Why do you care?" she mumbled in response before pulling out headphones and jamming them in her ears. In reality, she wished someone did care. Other than the meeting with Chad this morning, Jess had barely spoken with anyone. The truth was, she was lonely, but there was no way she would tell Emily that. She didn't need her making any more of a false effort to be friends when they had nothing in common.

"Hey."

The blonde's voice cut through her music, but Jess tried to ignore her, hoping she would leave her alone to wallow in her loneliness and dream of Chad, but she was persistent.

"Hey," she said again, tapping Jess's shoulder.

With a sigh, Jess pulled out one earphone and looked up at her. "What?" Her voice was flat and emotionless.

"I'm about to do my prayer time. I wanted to know if you'd like to join me or if I could pray for you in some way."

Her brown eyes appeared sincere as she waited for an answer, but Jess was unable to do more than blink at her. No one had ever offered to pray for her. Of course, since Jess didn't believe prayer worked, it had never mattered.

"No, I'm fine," she finally managed and shoved her earphone back in, but as the blonde shrugged and returned to her bed, Jess turned the volume down on her music. She wanted to hear what her prayer sounded like. Even though her mother had gone to church and claimed to be a Christian, Jess had never heard her pray.

The girl knelt in front of her bed and bowed her head. Her voice was soft as if speaking more to herself, and Jess had to strain to make out the words. "Dear Lord, I thank you for the blessings you have provided me. Thank you for the opportunity to make new friends.

You alone know the desires of our hearts, and I pray that you will touch Jess's heart and grant the desires of her heart. Lord also be with Jared. Give him peace and protect Nikki wherever she is. I pray for a hedge of protection on all of us this year so we may be examples for you and show love and grace as you do. Amen."

When she finished, the girl pushed herself up and sat down at the desk where she opened a large textbook probably to do homework. Slowly, Jess turned the music back up, but the girl's words ricocheted around in her head. She'd prayed for Jess even though she hadn't asked her to and yet not for herself. Wasn't that what Christians used prayer for? To ask God to give them things? Yet Emily had prayed for others and only asked to be a good example to others. A grey cloud of doubt filled Jess's head.

Could it be possible she had the wrong idea about Emily?

~

*E*mily was gone when Jess woke the next morning, so she figured it was time to put the tactics she had brainstormed into place. After listening to Emily pray the previous night and wrestling with feelings she didn't want most of the night, Jess decided there was no way she was as good as she seemed.

After dressing and brushing her teeth, Jess scattered piles of clothes around the room. Then, she opened a few of her granola bars and tossed the wrappers on Emily's bed. It wasn't much, but Jess had more planned for the afternoon when she returned. Grabbing her bag and chomping on a granola bar, she headed off to Biology, hoping it would be less boring than math had been the day before. Maybe, if she were lucky, she'd have another hot teacher like Chad to stare at.

~

*D*isgust flooded Jess's veins when she opened the door to the room that afternoon. Emily had picked up all the mess and folded the clothes, placing them neatly on Jess's bed. She now sat calmly at her desk working on something.

"Don't touch my stuff again," Jess spat at her, slamming the door and crossing to the bed to knock the perfectly piled clothes over. She pushed them with such intensity that some flew off the bed and landed on the floor.

"Don't leave such a mess, and I won't have to." Her voice was matter-of-fact, and her eyes never lifted from her book.

"Don't tell me what to do; you're not my mother," Jess snapped. How could she be so calm? It was infuriating. She picked up a few articles still on the bed, walked to the middle of the room, and purposefully dropped them.

Emily looked up and said with a sigh, "No, but I'm trying to be your friend. Look, I talked to the RA, but all the rooms are full. Even if I wanted to go, there's no place, so we are stuck with each other for the semester at least. We don't have to like each other, but we could try to get along."

"Or you could find a place off campus to live." Time for the next step. Jess opened the window and pulled out her pack of cigarettes. Clicking the lighter, she lit up and puffed. Though most of the smoke was going outside, she knew at least a little was seeping back into the room.

Emily coughed. "Excuse me, but there's no smoking in here. You need to take that outside."

"It's a free country," Jess said. "If you don't like it, you can leave."

Emily took a deep breath and forced a smile on her face. "I already told you I can't. I can't afford an apartment. My scholarship is paying for my dorm room." She stared at Jess a moment, then closed her eyes. Her lips moved though the words she was saying were too quiet for Jess to make out.

"What are you doing?" Jess asked. *Is she putting a curse on me?* Jess saw no voodoo doll, but she would put nothing past religious nut jobs.

Her eyelids opened, and her brown eyes met Jess's in a piercing gaze. "I'm praying for you. For us, really. We will have to live together at least this semester, and I can't make peace alone, so I'm praying for patience and for guidance."

A loud snort escaped Jess's lips. "Yeah, well good luck with that." She finished the cigarette and flicked the butt out the window. Music and messes hadn't worked, smoking hadn't worked, that left men. She would see Chad tomorrow when she had Psychology again. She would just have to work her magic on him.

CHAPTER 3

*J*ess's eyes snapped open. Something wasn't right. It was too bright. Glancing down at her watch, she uttered a quick curse before bounding out of bed. She had overslept and would be late. Any other day, it wouldn't have mattered, but today was Psychology again, and she didn't want to miss a minute of staring at beautiful Chad.

A quick look in the mirror revealed an

acceptable package. So, after a quick finger-comb of her hair, she hastily brushed her teeth, grabbed her books, and ran out the door. Though she didn't want to be out of breath when she arrived, she needed to walk at a quick pace or she would miss the first few minutes. As Jess trekked across the campus to the Psychology building, she wondered if it had been long enough that she could use Chad's number now. The loneliness was settling in, and some male company seemed liked the perfect remedy.

A glance at her wrist showed two minutes till class started. Jess quickened her pace and slid into a seat just seconds before Chad walked into the room. Taking a deep breath to calm her thudding heart, she smiled at him. She had chosen a seat closer to the front this time to see him better and so he would be sure to see her.

As he lectured, Jess tried to take notes, but her pen found its way to her mouth and her mind kept removing Chad's button-down shirt and revealing a six-pack of abs she longed to run her fingers over. Dropping her eyes, she tried to think of something else, anything else, to keep her obvious attraction from blazing like a marquee across her face.

The minutes seemed to both fly by and crawl at the same time. After her fourteenth glance at the clock, she began to fidget in her seat. Why couldn't the minute hand move faster? Jess wanted to catch up with Chad after class like she had on Monday.

When the class finally ended, Jess took her time gathering her things, hoping not to look too obvious. The door closed behind the last student, and she bounded down the front two rows and smiled at him. "Care for a smoke today?"

He looked up at her, his eyes traveling her body and taking in her tight shorts and black crop top. Jess was glad she had the figure to get away with them. "Actually, I've got the afternoon off," he smiled, "how would you like a private study session?"

She licked her lips, knowing exactly what he meant with his innuendo. His mind was certainly on the same track as hers. "I could definitely use one. I keep getting distracted because the teacher is so hot."

"Is that right?" he asked, matching her seductive tone. "Well then, your place or mine?"

Jess paused for a moment because she didn't know Emily's schedule yet. While she wanted to annoy Emily, she also wanted to make sure this happened. If

Emily were already in the room, it might not. "Let's do your place. I have the roommate from Hades, and I don't know if she'll be there or not."

He chuckled. "Yeah, I remember those days. So glad to have a single now."

"Yeah, they were supposed to get me one, but some idiot in their office screwed up."

"All right, come on." He locked the door, and Jess walked with him out into the sunshine. Math would have to take a back seat today, but she figured that was okay as she would be practicing a little addition anyway.

Chad didn't speak on the trek to his building, but Jess didn't care. Visions of what was coming filled her head and sent her pulse racing. As they entered the building, Chad grabbed his mail and headed up the stairs. Jess hurried behind him. He stopped outside room 212 and pulled out his keys. Jess swallowed the emotion in her throat; this was really going to happen! After opening the door, he held out his arm in a gesture for her to go first.

His room was like a small apartment. A private bathroom was on the left and a small kitchenette on the right. The main hallway opened to a living room with a door off to the left. A big screen TV hung on the wall of the living room, and a battered brown couch sat across from it. A small table was to the left of the couch.

"Just drop your bag there," he said pointing at the couch, before turning to another small table in the kitchenette.

Jess tossed her bag on the couch and turned around to come face to face with Chad's chest. He had dropped his mail and then closed the distance between them when she had been facing the other way. His arms wrapped around her waist and his eyes bore into her soul. Jess could get lost in those blue depths.

He dropped his head, and his lips crushed hers. Jess eagerly responded, following his lead as he walked her toward the door she had noticed earlier. Pushing it open with his back, Chad pulled Jess into the room and closed the door.

~

"Well, you certainly know how to make a girl's first week enjoyable," Jess said, smiling up at Chad from the crook of his arm.

He returned her smile, but conflicting emotions battled in his head. He had thought a romp with Jess would be just like every other fling he'd had for the last two years, but when he'd looked into her eyes, he'd felt something. Something like he used to feel when he dated before Kyle's death. And it scared him.

"Yeah, well, always happy to lend my services," he said. His hand traced a slow pattern on her shoulder as he thought about what to do. He needed to process and find a way to shut those feelings off again. "I should tell you though, I don't do relationships."

"I wasn't asking you to," she said, but he saw the flicker of hurt cross her face. A small part of him wanted to take his words back, but he was not a relationship guy. At least not since the death of his brother. Instead, he did what felt safest. He pushed her further away.

"Good," he said, "because while I'd love to do this again sometime, right now I need to get some work done." Chad stared at her, forcing his face to remain impassive.

A flush of embarrassment crawled

across Jess's face. "Oh, right, okay, sure." She rolled out of the bed and grabbed her clothes from the floor, pulling them on as fast as she could. "I'll uh just get out of your hair I guess."

"Thanks for understanding." Chad rolled out of bed and pulled on a pair of shorts. "If you want to get together again, call me, and if I don't hear from you before then, I'll see you next week in class."

"Sure, sounds good," Jess said, but Chad could tell she was forcing the brightness. Still, it was better this way. He needed to be upfront with her and let her know he was only looking for fun. He walked her to the front door, planted a quick kiss goodbye on her lips, and ushered her into the hallway.

As the door closed behind her, he leaned against it. What was going on with him? He never had feelings for the women he let come over, so why was he feeling something for Jess?

Across the room, his cell phone rang, dispelling thoughts of Jess for the moment, but as he picked up the phone and looked at the screen, he sighed. It was his mother. Though he didn't feel like talking to her, he couldn't ignore her call. She was hurting too and lonely with his father working all day, Kyle gone, and Kendra in school all day.

"Hi, Mom," he said as he clicked the answer call button.

"Hello, Son. How was your first week of teaching?" Her voice held the same false brightness he had detected in Jess's voice a few minutes ago.

"It was all right, I guess. It's a big class, so it should keep me busy."

"Have you made any new friends?"

Chad rolled his eyes. "Mom, it's college, not grade school."

"Sorry, I mean have you met anyone interesting?"

Just Jess he thought, but he wasn't telling his mother that. Though she probably suspected his philandering ways, she had never asked and he had never offered the information.

"It's the first week, Mom. I've been a little busy with instructing and keeping up with my own classes."

"Oh, well," she paused, "have you found a church?"

Chad sighed. They had this same discussion every time she called. "I'm not going to church, Mom. I told you that."

"It wasn't God's fault, Chad."

"Mom, we've been through this. Maybe you can still worship a God who lets your son get killed, but I can't. Look, I'm glad you called, but I need to get ready for a test on Monday." It wasn't the truth, but Chad couldn't handle any more guilt about not attending church.

"Okay, Son. I'll be praying for you."

"Sure, Mom." As Chad hung up the phone, he wondered if he'd ever get past his hurt and anger.

~

The door closed behind Jess, and a seed of disgust sprouted in her stomach. Why did she do this to herself? She knew nothing about Chad other than he was good looking, and yet she'd jumped right into bed with him.

A wave of anger boiled within her veins as she thought back to her most recent stepfather. He was the reason she did this. She hadn't been able to stop him from taking advantage of her, but once she'd found she could use sex to gain control in other relationships, the destructive pattern she'd been in the last few years had begun.

Unbidden, her thoughts wandered to Stephanie, and Jess wondered if she were okay. Stephanie was technically Jess's cousin, but when Stephanie's parents died in a car crash, Jess's mother had gained custody. While Jess had no love for the girl, she hadn't wanted Jim to turn his attention on her. He was certainly sick enough to do just that. She'd tried to warn Stephanie, but like Jess's mother, the girl hadn't believed her.

"You're wrong, you know? Jim would never do that," Stephanie said, *barging into Jess's room.* *"He's been such a great father to us."*

"I know you don't want to believe it," Jess said, *"but he does. That miscarriage I had? The baby was Jim's."*

Stephanie narrowed her eyes into slits and shook her head. "I don't believe you. You're obviously sleeping around to make yourself feel pretty. It's not our fault you couldn't narrow the father down."

Jess flinched at the hateful words. While she had begun sleeping around, it was only to erase the memory of carrying her stepfather's baby, even if only for a few weeks. "You don't know what you're talking about," Jess shot back, "but I'll be leaving for college soon and he'll have no one else. Do you think this was easy for me to tell you? I didn't ask for this. If you won't believe me, at least keep your guard up. Don't be alone with him and try to keep mom sober."

"You're disgusting. I'll be glad when you're gone," Stephanie said and stomped out of the room.

With a sigh, Jess pushed the memory away and headed down the hallway. Jim was no longer her problem. She'd closed that chapter of her life and had no intention of ever going back.

Emily looked up from her Bible as Jess entered the dorm room. Her mouth opened as if to speak, but then she closed it and dropped her eyes back to her Bible.

Thank God for small miracles. Jess grabbed her headphones from the bed and turned up the music. The pounding beats made it impossible to think, which was exactly what she needed.

CHAPTER 4

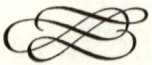

Friday was uneventful. As class ended, a part of Jess wanted to dial Chad's number to see if he was available. The other part of her still remembered the used feeling that enveloped her as he practically chased her from his room Wednesday. No, she might not have much dignity left, but she had enough not to call him this soon.

Jess didn't even stop at the front desk to check her mailbox as she entered the dorm. No one wrote to her, and her cell phone bill wasn't due yet. Though she didn't regret leaving home, she missed having someone to talk to. It wasn't like her mother had really listened in the last few years, but she had still been a warm body to throw words at. Some days, when Jim worked late and Stephanie wasn't around, they had watched movies together or baked cookies like old times.

She supposed she could have talked to Emily, but they had nothing in common besides being here on scholarship. No way could Jess tell her about Chad. Anyone who read their Bible and prayed as much as Emily did had no knowledge of lusty desires.

With a sigh, Jess stuck her key in the door and turned the knob, waiting for a barrage of questions about her day, but the room lay silent. Emily's bed was made but empty. Everything on her side of the room sat neatly in its place, as she always left it, but something was off.

Jess closed her eyes and pictured Emily's side of the room the way she had last seen it. The picture in her head scanned from left to right and when it reached Emily's nightstand, Jess's eyes popped open. Yes, there where her Bible usually sat, was an empty space. Since Jess doubted someone snuck into their room just to steal a Bible, she decided Emily must be off at some religious get-together.

As she dropped her bag on the bed, the desire to call Chad flared again. They would have the room to themselves, and if lucky, Emily might return while Chad was here, get offended, and leave for good.

Jess pulled her phone out of her pocket and swiped the screen, but as she clicked on the green phone icon, she paused. Calling today would make her appear desperate and nothing turned a guy off faster than desperation. In fact, the only thing worse than the used discarded feeling was the feeling of rejection. No, she could wait a few more days to dial his number. Play a little hard to get. She shoved the phone back in her pocket, plopped down on the bed, and punched the power button for the TV remote.

The TV hung on the wall, an older model that worked only because the dorm supplied free cable. Jess flicked past the news and the evening game shows, but on a Friday night not much else was on, unless she wanted to watch reruns of Full House or The Golden Girls, which she didn't.

She flicked the TV off. There was

always YouTube on her laptop, but Jess didn't feel like watching silly videos either. That left homework. There had been little assigned - being the first week of school - but she needed to catch up in the math class she had skipped. Jess pulled out the book and the syllabus, and after scanning for the missed assignment, she opened the book and tried to focus on the problems.

After reading the same problem three times, she closed the book and tapped her fingers on the cover. Entertainment! That's what she needed. This was a college town; surely a club existed near the campus.

Pushing the book aside, Jess stood up and grabbed her keys. After shoving her license, a credit card, and a twenty in the pocket of her shorts, she headed out the door, locking it behind her.

A mousy brunette with her face shoved in a book manned the information desk on the first floor. Though she looked like she could use it, Jess doubted she had ever stepped foot in a club, but her job was to know crap, so hopefully she had received good training.

"Hey," Jess said, tapping the desk to get her attention. The girl's eyes flicked up, but the book remained open, her index finger marking her stopping point. "Are there any local clubs around here that allow under twenty-ones?"

Her eyebrow inched up her forehead. "You have a phone?" she asked.

"Yeah."

"Then Google it." Her attention returned to her book.

"Thanks a lot," Jess said, though the words dripped with sarcasm. How that girl still had a job was beyond her. They must be desperate for help. Jess dug her cell phone from her pocket and pulled up a browser.

There were three clubs listed, but only one allowed underage entrance on Friday nights. The Hangout it was then. After plugging the address into her phone, Jess headed that direction.

The Hangout was a large brick building that looked like it had been a warehouse at some point. A large, muscled man with tattoos on his biceps, up his neck, and on his bald head stood at the door. Whether he was or not, he exuded a tough exterior and with his beefy arms crossed, he looked like a solid wall.

"ID please," he said as she approached.

Jess dug in her back pocket and pulled out her license. She no longer had her car, having sold it to have money for college expenses until she could get a job, but her license was still valid though rarely used now.

He perused it, flipped it over, and then handed it back. "It's a ten-dollar cover."

Jess nodded and pulled open the solid metal door. Another man, much smaller and wearing Buddy Holly type glasses stood behind a counter. She handed a twenty to him and he slid a ten-dollar bill back which she shoved in her pocket before scanning the room.

The room was large and open with a bar on the left and a dance floor in the middle, encased by a railing that separated it from the tables around the outside. Few people were on the dance floor yet as it was relatively early, but the music was blaring and lights lit up the floor.

Jess walked over to the bar and ordered a Diet Coke. She lounged on a barstool while she waited. A few minutes later, a glass slid in front of her and she sipped it as she watched the few people on the dance floor.

A girl with long brown dreads appeared lost in her own world, swaying slightly to the music while a chunky boy tried to gain the attention of the two blonde girls on the floor. They were adept at ignoring him, turning their back to him whenever he approached while making it appear they simply danced to the beat.

"You a people watcher?"

Jess turned to the bartender who leaned against the counter watching her watch the dance floor.

"Sometimes," she said with a shrug. "They're all basically the same though."

His brows knit together, "What do you mean?"

"I mean we all put on a show to get people to like us, but then our real colors come out and we just end up hurting each other."

He let out a low whistle. "Well, that's a very pessimistic view of the world. You seem a little young to be so jaded."

"It is what it is." She finished the drink and pushed it back to him. He had no idea what was in her past nor did he have the right to judge her. "Have a good night." Suddenly, she didn't want to stay here with the intuitive bartender and the sparse crowd.

"Anytime," he hollered as she walked away. "I'm here every weekend."

~

*C*had looked at Jess's number in his phone. After the long week, he could use another release, but he wasn't sure he wanted to call her. Though he'd definitely enjoyed his time with her, he hadn't enjoyed the feelings she brought up in him. He wasn't looking for long-term.

Long-term could lead to love and people you loved died. It was easier not to go near it.

No, he didn't need Jess. He needed a ride. Shoving his phone back in his pocket, he grabbed his helmet and headed downstairs.

The evening was perfect for a ride, clear and warm. He mounted the Harley and let the engine hum for a minute, enjoying the aggressive vibration of the engine. Then he pulled on his helmet, swung his leg over the bike, and released the brake.

The speed limit on campus was slow, but University Avenue loomed ahead and shortly beyond that - the interstate where he could ramp up past the speed limit. As he idled at the stoplight, a woman across the street caught his eye. He couldn't see her face, but her short shorts showed off long lean legs, and her shirt hugged her figure in all the right places. She looked like she enjoyed a good time.

When the light turned green, he turned her direction and pulled the bike up to the shoulder just behind her. He flipped up his visor. "Care for a ride?"

She turned and his smile froze on his face. It was Jess. What were the odds?

A sexy smile lit up her face. "Sure," she said. "I'm always up for a ride."

Who was Chad to deny fate? It obviously wanted them together tonight. He reached behind him and grabbed the spare helmet he kept attached to the back of the bike for just such occasions.

She took it from him, smoothing her raven locks back as she pulled it on.

"I don't have a spare coat," he said. Though the night was warm, the breeze would get chilly as they rode.

"That's all right, you can warm me up later." As she swung up behind him and laced her arms around his waist, the scent of some exotic perfume wafted over his shoulder. When he was sure she was secure, he throttled the bike, and they roared off into the setting sun.

CHAPTER 5

*J*ess's eyes snapped open at the presence of someone beside her in the bed. Chad's stubbled chin filled her view and she smiled. Then the memory of their last encounter crashed back in. He had let her stay the night, but without a doubt he would ask her to leave as soon as he woke and she wanted to avoid being dismissed again.

As quietly as possible, Jess slid out of the bed and dressed. With a final glance

Chad's direction, she slipped out of the room. At least this way, she kept the power.

"Early breakfast?" Emily asked as Jess entered the room.

"Good night," Jess answered with a smile, deciding to make Emily as uncomfortable as possible. "I guess you did too since you were out late yourself. At least you weren't back by the time I left."

"I did," Emily said with a sweet smile, ignoring the innuendo. "Friday nights I have a Bible study with some friends. You could join us some week if you'd like."

"I'd rather get teeth pulled," Jess returned, crossing to the sink to grab her shower items. Of course Emily was off doing something religious. Did the girl do nothing else with her life?

After a quick shower, Jess returned to the room and dressed. It was Saturday, and she had nothing to do. Perhaps it was time to find a job. Not that she wanted to work, but the money from her savings and the sale of her car would only last so long.

Jess smoothed her hair down and headed out the door. Plenty of businesses lined the campus. Surely one of them would be hiring.

The first shop she entered was a bookstore that also sold Tech merchandise. Jess made her way to the back counter where a girl about her age worked the counter. Unfortunately, she was clearly a preppy cheerleader type. Biting the inside of her lip, Jess forced a smile on her face.

"Hi, is there an application I could fill out?" Jess asked when she reached the counter.

The blonde cocked her head and flashed a smile that oozed pity. "Oh, I'm sorry. We aren't hiring right now. If you have a resume, I'd be happy to leave it with the manager."

Resume. Of course, why hadn't she thought to bring a resume? Maybe because she didn't have much work experience. She'd worked her Junior and Senior year at the one and only gas station in Paducah, but that was the extent of her job history and it wasn't impressive.

"Um, I forgot to bring one with me, but can I drop it by later?" Jess asked.

"Sure," the girl said.

Jess received the same story at the next five places she tried and two hours later, she returned to the dorm tired and worried. If she couldn't find a job soon, she didn't know what she would do.

"Hey," Jess cleared her throat - She couldn't believe she was about to ask Emily for help - "Do you know of any place that is hiring? I need to get a job."

Emily looked up from the book she was reading and studied Jess. "My friend Jared works at the Student Union. I think he said they were hiring. Do you want me to check with him?"

"Yeah, I guess that'd be cool," Jess said with a shrug. What was with this girl? She had been nothing but rude to Emily and she was still willing to help.

"Okay, hang on."

As Emily tapped out a message on her phone, the question that had been burning in Jess's brain burst forth. "Why are you willing to help me?"

She flashed a small smile. "Look, I won't say you've been super easy to live with, but I try to find the good in everyone. I don't know what pain you've dealt with in your past, but I know that God can heal it if you ask Him."

"I appreciate your help in finding a

job, but I don't need your sales pitch on God," Jess said.

"Fair enough," Emily said with a shrug, dropping the subject. A moment later her phone chimed. "Okay, he's there now and said he can get you a face to face with the director."

"Uh, sure," Jess said. "That would be great." She followed Emily out of the room, surprised that she had been willing to drop the topic of God so quickly. Emily seemed different from the other Christians Jess had met. They had tried to push God on her at every turn and one had even told her she was signing her ticket to Hell if she didn't convert. What made Emily so different?

The campus was bustling with activity as they made their way to the Student Union building. Games of Frisbee and flag football filled the open spaces and individuals lounged against tree trunks reading in the shade.

Emily pulled open the doors of the student union, and the quiet engulfed Jess. Due to the nice weather, most people were outside and not sitting in buildings. With a purposeful stride, Emily led the way to the cafe where evidently Jared worked.

The cafe too was quiet with only a few people seated at tables around the room, but as they entered, an average-looking male with brown hair approached.

"Hey, Emily," he said before turning to face Jess. "Jess?" he asked, holding out his hand.

She nodded and shook his hand. "Yeah."

He glanced at Emily with a raised brow.

"What she means to say," Emily said,

shooting a pointed look Jess's direction, "is thank you for helping her out."

"Right," Jess mumbled. "Thank you for helping me out." Few people in her life had offered such kindness, and she still wasn't sure how to process the feelings battling within her.

"Anything for a friend of Emily's," he said.

Jess opened her mouth to correct him, but thought better of it and smiled instead. Emily had probably already told him about her and therefore he was either being sarcastic or trying to be nice, and she didn't want to know if it was the former.

"Okay, well I leave you in good hands," Emily said. "I'll be praying you get the job."

Before Jess could say anything, Emily walked away, leaving her standing awkwardly with Jared.

"All right, well Darla is probably in her office. Follow me and I'll take you there."

Darla was a short, curvy woman with dark hair and red lips. She looked up from her desk as Jared knocked on the door.

"Hey, Darla," he said. "This is my friend Jess. She's looking for a job. Do we have anything open?"

"I don't know," she said with a smile, "but if Jared vouches for you, I'll take a look. Come on in."

Jess followed Jared inside, feeling like a charlatan as she sat beside him. They weren't friends; she had just met him. Why was he putting his name on the line for her?

"Let's see," Darla said, clicking the buttons on her mouse. "Well, I have an opening in food service in the cafe."

"Um." Jess needed a job, but she wasn't sure she could work in food service.

Darla laughed. "Yeah, it's not for everyone. Hmm, let's see. Well, the only other thing I have is a mail clerk position. You'd pick up the mail, sort it by departments, and then deliver it. There might be light filing as well. It's only ten hours a week though."

It was not her dream job, but Jess had no desire to return home to beg for money nor did she feel like losing her cell phone for non-payment or starving. Plus, the job sounded solitary, her specialty. "Thank you, I think it would be fine. Is there an application?"

Darla smiled and slid a piece of paper across the desk. "The application is merely a formality. I do have to run a background check, but I'm willing to take a chance on you."

Jess squirmed in her seat, feeling a smidgen of guilt for the false image Darla had of her, but she needed this job, and though she had plenty of other faults, she was reliable. Quickly, Jess scribbled down her information and passed the sheet back to Darla.

After taking a copy of her license, Darla shook Jess's hand. "I should have the background check back by Monday afternoon, so how about we plan to start on Tuesday? If something comes up on your report that would affect your employment, I'll call you Monday evening."

"That sounds great," Jess agreed. There was plenty of bad in her past, but it had all been done *to* her, and though she had technically broken the law drinking and smoking before she was legally old enough, she had never been caught.

As Jess followed Jared out of the office, her curiosity got the better of her, and she grasped his arm. "Why did you do this for me? You don't even know me, and I haven't been very nice to Emily."

His kind eyes studied her face. "I know, Emily talked a little about you last night at Bible study, but she also said you needed help and that's what we are here to do."

"You're one too," Jess said as the realization dawned on her.

"If you mean a believer," he said with a chuckle, "yeah I am."

"Well, thanks," Jess said.

Jess spent the rest of Saturday trying to sort through her feelings of confusion. Emily was like no one she had ever met, and though she'd only met Jared the one time, he appeared to be just like Emily. The two of them were calling into question every judgement Jess had made about Christians.

By evening, she wanted a distraction. Her hand reached for her phone to call

Chad, but she froze before dialing. She had just seen him last night. Would he consider this too soon? With a sigh, she put the phone down and opened her laptop, but after a few minutes of scrolling aimlessly, she closed the lid and grabbed her phone again. It might be too soon, but Jess needed to get her mind off Emily and Chad was the only way she knew how to do it.

"I only have a few hours," he said over the phone. "I have plans later."

His words cut like a knife, reminding her that she was nothing more than a release for him, but she was too confused to care.

"That's fine," she shot back. "I have plans too."

Fifteen minutes later, Chad was in her room and five minutes after that, they were in her bed. As soon as his lips touched hers, Jess's confusion flew out the window.

For the moment, her thoughts were consumed with his chiseled body and luscious lips. That is until the door opened.

"What are you doing?" Emily gasped from the doorway. "This is my room too. You can't do this here!"

"Actually, she can," Chad spoke up.

"I don't need to hear from you," Emily said, turning angry eyes on him.

Jess had never seen Emily angry, and after her help earlier this afternoon, Jess suddenly felt awful.

"I'm going to get dinner," Emily said, focusing her angry eyes back on Jess. "I want him gone when I get back."

The door slammed behind Emily, and Jess turned to Chad. "Maybe you should go."

"Yeah, whatever, the mood is ruined anyway and you're right. Your roommate is a piece of work."

Jess shrugged, unwilling to agree with him but not wanting to explain her change of heart.

As they dressed, an enormous guilt descended on Jess's shoulders. She often felt used and disgusted with herself after intimacy, but this was the first time she felt guilty. Was it simply because Emily had been so nice to her or was there some other reason?

"Next time my place, okay, babe?" Chad asked as he pulled open the door.

Jess nodded distractedly as she returned the quick kiss he planted on her before sauntering off down the hall. After the door closed behind Chad, Jess returned to her bed and curled her knees to her chest. Slowly her guilt turned to anger. Emily had no right to embarrass her like that, and she had no right to tell Jess she couldn't entertain a man in the room. She paid just as much for the room as Emily did.

By the time Emily returned, Jess had worked herself into quite a tizzy. "What's your problem?" she demanded when Emily entered.

She sighed as she dropped her wallet on the desk. "My problem is that I live here too. If you want to engage in that behavior that's your deal but I don't want to be a witness to it."

"You can't tell me I can't have him here," Jess spat back.

"That's true," she said calmly, "but I can ask you to respect my position, and I can tell you that he can't fill the void you have."

"You know nothing about me." Jess's hands curled into fists at her side, but she found herself angrier that Emily was right. How many times had she used sex to fill the feeling of emptiness inside her only to feel even emptier afterwards?

"Not for lack of trying," Emily said as she sat on her bed. "I've been trying to get to know you all week, but you keep pushing me away."

Jess wanted to hurl more hateful words at her, but none came to mind. With an angry huff, she shoved her earphones in and turned up the music. Emily was stirring up all kinds of feelings she didn't want to deal with.

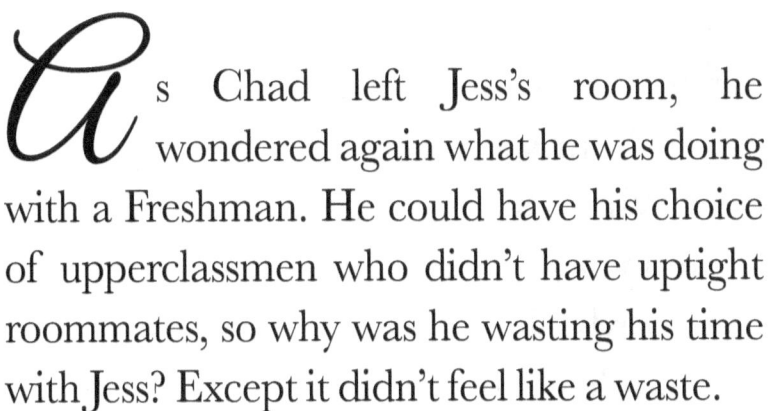

*A*s Chad left Jess's room, he wondered again what he was doing with a Freshman. He could have his choice of upperclassmen who didn't have uptight roommates, so why was he wasting his time with Jess? Except it didn't feel like a waste.

Every time he was with her, he felt…. different. Not so angry or something. He ran a hand across his jaw and shook his head. What was he thinking? The last thing he needed was to be falling for some woman. No, what he actually needed was a stiff drink. Something to clear his head.

Chad had never been much of a drinker, at least not until Kyle was killed. After Kyle's death, he had turned from prayer to the bottle. Tequila didn't solve everything, but it dulled the ache of missing his brother.

Instead of heading toward his dorm, Chad turned toward University Avenue. Bruno's was open early and often had happy hour specials.

"What can I get for you, hon?" The bartender wore a tight fitting shirt with the words 'Liquor is my passion' across her ample chest.

"Shot of Tequila," Chad answered as he slid onto the upholstered barstool.

"Little early to be drinking, isn't it?" she asked as she turned to grab a glass.

"Not if you need to do thinking," he replied.

"I'm a good listener if you need ears," she said with a wide smile as she placed the glass in front of him.

Chad gave her another once over. She was pretty though she wore a little too much make up for his taste. However, she could probably distract him from Jess if he needed the distraction. "Thanks, I'll keep that in mind," he said with a wink as he picked up the glass and downed the shot.

CHAPTER 6

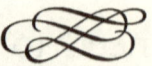

*J*ess was still processing Emily's behavior the next morning when she woke up. Emily lay in her bed reading from the Bible. Though Jess had seen nothing useful when she had glanced through it, something must keep drawing Emily back.

She bit her lip as she watched Emily. Even after the hateful words Jess had spewed at her, Emily had stayed calm and resolute. She seemed to believe in something rather than trying to be perfect or pushy like other religious people Jess had met.

"Why do you read the Bible every day?" The words escaped Jess's lips before she could stop them.

Emily glanced up, a look of surprise on her face. "Well, partly because God told us to, and partly because it gives me peace. If something is ever bothering me, I can usually find peace in the Bible."

"What do you mean? What peace? The only time I ever looked in one, I found it confusing."

She chuckled and nodded. "Yes, some parts of it are confusing, but it's also one of God's ways of communicating with us."

Jess chewed on her bottom lip, trying to understand what Emily meant. "You mean like I ask it a question and let it fall open and I'll find the answer?"

Emily shook her head. "No, it rarely

works like that. It's not a Magic 8 ball. What I mean is, the more you read it, the more things will become clear to you. Sometimes you might read something that answers a question you have, but sometimes you'll read something about trusting people and a friend will tell you what you need to hear or you'll read something that makes you pray for something or someone."

She paused and pursed her lips. Then her face lit up. "Here, I've got an example. My parents wanted a baby, but for some reason, they couldn't conceive. One day, after praying with their pastor at church, they passed a woman heading into an abortion clinic. My mother blurted out to the woman that she wanted her baby, and the woman paused and turned to them. She told my parents she had been wrestling with the decision to have an abortion and had asked God for a sign not to do it. You see, my mother calling out to her was that sign, and my mother is a very shy person. Calling out like that wasn't in her normal nature at all. That's a pretty big coincidence, don't you think?" Emily's eyes danced as she finished the story.

Jess didn't know what to think, but she found herself wanting to believe it, to grasp onto something that might make sense in her messed-up life. "Were you that baby?"

"I was," Emily said.

"Didn't you ever hate your mother? I mean doesn't it bother you that she didn't want you?"

Emily shook her head. "No, don't you see? My mother thought she was trapped. She couldn't afford to have a baby, and the man had left tread marks in his departure from her life when she told him she was pregnant, so she felt all alone. I'm one of the lucky ones. My mother wrestled with the decision and prayed about it rather than rushing into it, and God saw fit to send my parents into her path. If they hadn't crossed paths that day, I wouldn't be here today."

"Does your faith really give you peace?" Jess asked. Though peace seemed foreign with her stained past, the thought was appealing.

"Yes, but just reading the Bible won't give you peace if you don't know Jesus. The peace comes from Him. Would you like me to tell you some about Him?"

Something deep inside Jess screamed 'yes,' but her pragmatic mind still wouldn't accept it. She felt the wall going back up. "No, I don't have time for stuff like that. I just wondered why you spent so much time reading."

Emily stared a moment longer, then

she shrugged and turned back to her book.

"Hey, it's Sunday, shouldn't you be at church or something?"

Emily glanced down at her watch and frowned. "Yeah, I should be. Jared should be picking me up soon, but I guess he's running late."

"So that's your kryptonite?"

"Huh?" she asked.

"Your weakness. Going places alone? I wondered what it was. You seemed so perfect, but I knew there had to be something."

Emily smiled. "Well, first off, I am not perfect. I've never claimed to be. I'm just trying to do God's will, but yeah, walking alone into crowded places is pretty much my worst nightmare."

Jess regarded her for a second, feeling a little bad. "Well, I hope he shows up."

"You know, you could come with me," she said.

"I don't do church." Jess reached for her headphones. It was time to end this discussion.

"Have you tried?" she asked. "Look, all I'm saying is that whatever you're looking for, men probably can't supply. But Jesus? He can heal any pain you're feeling."

Jess snorted and rolled her eyes. "Yeah, Jesus has never been there for me. I've always had to look out for myself."

"Have you ever asked Him?"

She opened her mouth to reply but shut it again. A knock sounded at the door.

"That will be Jared," Emily said with a small sigh, "but I hope we can talk again soon." Her voice held a hint of sadness, as if she were almost considering staying to finish the conversation, but after a final glance Jess's direction, she grabbed her Bible and left.

Jess glared ice at the closed door. Emily didn't know her. But even as the words formed in her mind, she realized at least a bit of it was true. Jess didn't have any close friends, and whenever loneliness struck, she did turn to men for comfort, though the comfort only stayed while the men were there. Still, that didn't mean she was easy or whatever Emily had been implying.

Jess flopped back on the bed, but the silence inched in on her. She tapped her fingers against the mattress and tried to think of something to take her mind off the loneliness. She had some homework; maybe she could do that.

Pulling out her Psychology book, she opened it up to the chapter they were supposed to read, but the only thing popping up was Chad's face. With a sigh,

Jess slammed the book shut, rolled over, and fished Chad's number out of the nightstand drawer.

Want to meet up? She tapped the message in the phone but then paused, trying to decide if she really wanted to send it. Desperation never looked good on anyone and they had gotten together Friday and Saturday. Her finger hovered over the send button, and ever so stealthily it tapped send. No taking it back now.

The seconds dragged on as Jess waited for the return bubble, and the screen timed out and darkened. With an agitated swipe, she turned it on again. How long did it take to reply? The phone beeped. *Sorry, can't right now* popped up on the screen. Disgust boiled in Jess's stomach, and she tossed the phone down. What good was a friend with benefits if he wasn't available when she needed him? As the nervous energy built inside her, she paced back and forth in the room and decided she needed a smoke.

~

C had pushed the guilt away as he sent the text dismissing Jess. She was lonely and he knew it, but seeing her three days in a row felt like starting a relationship and he couldn't do it. Besides, he needed to prepare for classes the next day.

The Psychology class had a quiz coming up that he needed to write, but as he sat down at his desk, Jess's face kept popping into his head. The sadness in her blue eyes and the feel of her skin against his plagued his mind. She reminded him of himself and he wondered what pain was in her past.

He reached for his cell phone and

paused. If he texted Jess, he would be sending her all the wrong signals. No, it could wait. He could wait, but he couldn't deny he enjoyed being around her - more than he had any woman in the past two years.

Placing the cell phone to the side, he turned back to the Psychology book, but his mind and his eyes wandered to the phone every few minutes. He wondered what Jess was doing. Ugh, he would never get his work done this way.

Slamming the book closed, Chad grabbed his keys and headed out the door, deliberately leaving his phone on the desk. If he didn't have it, he couldn't be tempted to call Jess, but maybe a ride would clear his head enough to focus.

CHAPTER 7

"What is the matter with you?" Chad asked, propping himself up on his elbow and causing his biceps to bulge. Though he hadn't been available yesterday when Jess had texted, he had responded this morning, and offered to come over after class. Since she knew Emily would be in class, she agreed.

His blue eyes stared down at her, expecting an answer she didn't have. She should be into this. He was built like a god, and the light sheen of sweat glistening on his body made his muscles appear to ripple, but as Jess lay beneath him, all she could think about were Emily's words - that men couldn't fill the hole in her heart, but Jesus could.

Jess shook her head as she looked back at Chad. He was handsome, but she knew nothing about him, other than he was a TA, rode a motorcycle, and stirred lustful emotions in her body. And while the immediate pleasure was nice, the void always remained when he left, and with it came the fear. Fear of pregnancy, fear of STDs, fear of labeling. Jess had been used for so long that her self-respect now depended on a man's attention. The worst part was it rarely even mattered which man.

"I'm sorry," she said, trying to clear the thoughts. "It's just something my roommate said."

"The prude who walked in on us the other day?" He knitted his dark brows together. "Who cares what she thinks?" He leaned in to kiss Jess again, but her hand pushed him back. Her traitorous hand. What was it doing? She should let him kiss her and allow the pleasurable sensation to overwhelm her, but she couldn't. Her mouth followed her hand's actions, speaking without permission.

"I know, it's just... what's your favorite food?"

"My favorite what? Never mind." He pushed himself up, and his blue eyes bored into hers. His mouth opened as if to say something, then closed. With a shake of his head, he stood "This just got too real. I'm not looking for a relationship, just an easy hook-up. Call me again when you're ready for that, otherwise, don't call me." He lumbered off the bed and pulled his clothes back on.

After flashing one last incredulous look, he left the room.

The emptiness crowded in worse than before as Jess retrieved her own clothes. *Stupid, stupid, stupid. Why did you do that?* As she yanked on her shorts, hatred simmered in her stomach for Emily. She had been at peace with her life before Emily's words dug in and took hold. Sure, it hadn't been great, but she had learned how to cope with it. Why hadn't she gotten the single she had asked for? If she had, this never would have happened. This was all that goody-two-shoes's fault, and Jess wanted to make Emily pay.

After pulling on her shirt, she glanced over at Emily's side of the room. What could she do to her that would send Emily into a tailspin like she was in? She could tear down her pictures or deface them, but Emily would just get more. No, that was too easy; it needed to be something bigger, something that would hurt her more. Jess's eyes landed on the Bible. If she tore it to pieces that would hit Emily; she was always reading the bloody thing.

Stomping to the nightstand, Jess reached for the book, but a heat blazed against her hand. Jerking it back, she stared at the book, and her heart thudded in her chest. What was that? She had touched it before and felt nothing. Jess stepped away from the book and returned to her bed. Pulling her knees up to her chest, she stared at the black book that now held an unexplainable power and tried not to panic.

⌇

I have to end this, Chad thought as he left Jess's room. *She's getting attached.* He knew the signs. He'd seen it in many of the girls over the last two years. Normally, this would be the time he would stop calling the girl, pretend to lose her number, and find another one. It's what he should do with Jess, but he couldn't. He couldn't keep her piercing blue eyes and soft lips from re-entering his brain. He needed time away from her. Away from the feelings she was stirring in his heart.

The best way he knew to do that was to find another woman. Someone he didn't have feelings for. Maybe the bartender from Bruno's he had met the other night. Though not his usual type, she was pretty and had seemed attracted to him.

He was heading that direction when his phone rang. Pulling it out, he looked at the number. The area code was the same as his hometown's but he didn't recognize the number.

"Hello?" he said, punching the button.

"Hi, Chad, it's Amy. Can you talk?"

His heart dropped to his stomach. Amy had been Kyle's girlfriend and a staple at their house before Kyle's death, but Chad hadn't spoken with her since the funeral. However, he knew she was still attending church with his parents and kept in touch with his mother.

"I have studying and planning to do," he said with a sigh, forgetting the blonde bartender. "What do you need?"

"Actually, I think it might be something you need. Can you come home this weekend?"

Chad avoided going home except for major holidays, summers, and when his mother begged him. Mostly it was to avoid memories of Kyle, but also it was because his parents always insisted on dragging him to church. Chad had given up God when Kyle's casket was lowered into the ground.

"Please. I think you need to see this," Amy said when Chad hesitated.

His curiosity got the better of him. "Fine. I'll be there on Saturday."

~

"Whoa, you look like you've seen a ghost." Emily said when she returned that afternoon.

Jess looked at her and then glanced over at the Bible. "What's in that book?" Though her voice sounded calm, her heart still beat erratically in her chest.

Emily's brow wrinkled, "What book?"

"Your Bible." Jess pointed, feeling eerily like the ghost of Christmas Future. Her hand trembled slightly.

Emily crossed to the Bible and picked

it up. "I've already told you. God's instructions to help us live. Why?"

"I wanted to destroy it," Jess began mechanically.

Emily's eyes widened. "Why?"

"You got in my head with your words and I may have ruined things with Chad because of it. I wanted to hurt you, but when I went to touch it, heat flared against my hand. What sort of voodoo magic is that?"

"It's not voodoo," Emily sighed, shaking her head. "It was God. He's trying to get your attention. He loves you, and he wants you to come home."

The words pierced Jess's heart. "No one has ever loved me, and I don't have a home any longer." Tears pricked her eyes as images of the day she left home flooded into her mind:

"Where do you think you're going?" her mother asked, hands akimbo, brown hair wild

and frizzy. The smell of alcohol radiated from her pores and her eyes couldn't seem to focus.

"I'm leaving," Jess replied, shoving clothes into her large duffle. "I have to get away from him. I can't stay here and watch him do to his own daughter what he did to me."

"What are you talking about? He's been a great father to you since we married, and he's taking care of us."

Jess's knuckles whitened as she clutched the shirt she was packing even tighter. "No father should do to a daughter what he does, and the only thing he's taking care of is your drug habit."

Her mother's eyes narrowed as she stumbled across the room and slapped Jess's face. "How dare you! Why would he even want anything from you? Look at yourself; you're so ugly. And you're always whoring around. Why would he want that?"

Tears stung Jess's eyes, both from the physical slap and from the emotional pain of the cutting words from the one person she thought loved her.

"I can't believe you would side with him over me. I only started sleeping around after my miscarriage. That baby was your husband's by the way. But why should you believe me? I'm just your daughter."

"I don't have a daughter," her mother spat and faltered from the room, grabbing the walls to steady her gait.

Jess let the tears flow as she finished shoving what she could in the big black bag. With a final glance around the room, she slung the bag on her shoulder and left the house she had called home for eighteen years.

Emily pulled the desk chair around and sat in it facing Jess. "First off, I'm sure someone has loved you, even if it doesn't often feel like it. Second, God has loved you forever. He knit you together in your mother's womb, and he knew every hair on your head then and now. He sent his only son, Jesus, to die for your sins so you could spend eternity in Heaven with Him.

So, you do have a home, a heavenly home, and even though you can't go there now, one day you will get to see it in all its glory. Our life here on earth is so fleeting. It's important to remember that even though life here will not always be what we expected, what's coming next makes it worth it."

"Do you really believe that?" Jess asked. She wanted to believe—there had to be more to life than what she'd seen so far—but there had been so many hurts, so much pain.

"With all my heart." Her serious tone matched the intensity blazing out of her eyes.

"I'll think about it." Jess rolled over and stared at the wall, but her mind replayed Emily's words over and over again.

CHAPTER 8

*J*ess sighed as she stared at the empty room. Emily was out, probably with Jared and the rest of her group again. She had told Jess about the others over the last few days, and while she'd invited Jess along, Jess wasn't sure she was ready to be immersed in Emily's crowd yet.

On top of that, Jess had been avoiding Chad all week, and he hadn't called either. Her old habit would have been to go out to a club, pick up a handsome man, and bring him back home, but every time she dressed for that occasion, her stomach would clench up and Emily's words would parade back through her head. Was God trying to get her attention?

From across the room, the black book called out like a beacon in a storm. Would it shock her again? Running her palms down denim clad thighs, she pushed herself up from the bed and crossed to Emily's nightstand. Jess's hand hovered over the book, but no heat licked at it this time. Had she imagined it last time? Tentatively, she dropped a finger to the cover. Nothing. Gathering the last of her courage, she placed her palm flat on the cover and closed her eyes.

A spark of light and the image of a cross filled her vision. Startled, Jess pulled her hand back and stared at the book. There was no pain, but why was she seeing visions? She had never seen visions before. Were they permanent? She held her breath and touched the book again. Nothing. No light, no cross, just the textured cover. Jess sat on Emily's bed, pulled her knees to her chest, and opened the book, deciding to look towards the end this time.

The red text jumped out at her. "I am the way, the truth, and the life. No man comes to the father except through me." She turned back a few pages. "For God so loved the world that he sent his one and only son that whoever believes in him shall not perish but have eternal life." Eternal life? Was this for real? Jess raised her brows but kept reading. "For God did not send his son into the world to condemn the world but to save the world through him. Whoever believes in him is not condemned, but whoever does not believe stands condemned already because he has not believed in the name of God's one and only son." Was she condemned? More importantly, if she was, could she change her fate? A desire to learn all she could filled her soul, and Jess eagerly turned back to the book.

The sound of the door opening interrupted Jess's reading, and she slammed the book shut and replaced it on Emily's nightstand. As she pushed herself up from the bed, she smoothed the comforter. Only a few wrinkles hinted at her intrusion on Emily's side, but Emily looked too preoccupied to notice.

"Whoa, what happened to you?" The normal smile that framed her heart-shaped face was missing and her flawless, olive skin appeared paler than usual.

Emily shuddered. "I just feel dirty. Some guy came up to me as we were leaving the restaurant and he practically undressed me with his eyes. I think I need a dozen showers." She shivered and rubbed her arms as she sat on the bed.

"Welcome to my world," Jess muttered.

"What do you mean?" Emily looked up, and her eyes were so sincere that a chunk of the wall Jess had built around her heart crumbled, and she found herself telling Emily about her stepfather. "Oh my gosh, Jess, I'm so sorry." Emily rose from her bed. She crossed the room and sat beside Jess.

Jess shrugged. "I'm kind of used to it. He wasn't the first, just the worst. The first time my mom fell to drugs, she hooked up with a real winner. He had a temper, so I never knew whether he was going to hit me or"—she stared down at her hands, embarrassed and let the sentence trail off.

"That is not okay. It should never have

happened to you. Is that why you're so...
guarded?"

"Maybe," Jess said, tracing a line on
her left palm with the thumb of her right
hand. "You're less likely to get hurt if you
keep walls up, you know?"

Emily's brown eyes stared into Jess's
with a blazing intensity. "I know you
aren't a believer, but can I pray for you?"

It was the second time Emily had
asked her, and while Jess still wasn't sure
she believed in prayer, Emily seemed to,
and her voice held a sense of urgency.
What could it hurt? Jess nodded, and
Emily bowed her head and closed her
eyes.

"Lord, my friend Jess is hurting
because of her past. Please heal her and
show her your love."

As Emily continued praying, Jess felt
another chunk of the wall she had so
carefully created crumble. Tears welled up

inside and threatened to overflow. She sniffed and ran a hand over her eyes, willing them to stay dry. The effort was futile. They spilled out, creating wet, shiny tracks down her cheeks. Her shoulders heaved as six years of hurt slammed against the dam, crumbling it to bits. When Emily finished praying, she grabbed Jess's hand

"Can he take it away?" Jess sobbed. "Can He make me forget my past?"

"Your past is always with you," Emily said. "But He can give you a brighter future. You don't have to be a slave to your past."

Suddenly Jess wanted that more than anything. She didn't know if Emily was telling the truth, but if there was even a possibility, she wanted it. "Tell me what to do. I want the peace you seem to have."

"Just ask God to save you. Tell him

you know you're a sinner and you want him to guide your life."

Jess said the words through tears, and when she finished, Emily hugged her. Though she was not generally a "huggy" person, she found her arms returning the embrace as a weird need to laugh bubbled inside.

A tiny chuckle escaped along with the words. "What do I do now?"

"Now you read. You learn everything you can, and you try to live it. I won't lie; it isn't always easy, but it's always worth it."

"What about the emptiness? I still feel it."

"You have to give that to God. It won't go away instantaneously, but He will begin to fill it, if you let Him."

Jess nodded, smiling at Emily and enjoying the lighter feeling. Though the emptiness remained, it felt like a heavy blanket had been lifted from her shoulders.

"Hey, will you come to church with me Sunday?" Emily asked. "There's a really great college crowd at my church."

Jess nodded, almost mechanically, but her mind wondered if she would be accepted with her shaved hair and nose ring?

~

*C*had's throat grew dryer the closer he got to Amarillo. He had been home a few times in the summer, but as his dorm allowed him to stay on campus during the summer, he had claimed his summer work of clerking at a counselor's office kept him stuck in Lubbock and had avoided spending much time at home.

Though he was coming into town to see Amy, he knew he would have to make at least a quick stop at his parent's house, but he decided to do it on the way out of town.

He was surprised to see a moving van in front of Amy's house when he pulled up. Intrigued, he locked the car and walked up the steps. Before his hand even hit the doorbell, the door swung open.

"Oh, hello, Chad," Amy's mother said from the other side. While he hadn't spent much time here, Amy's parents had often joined them for dinner and festivities when Kyle was living. The last two years had added a few streaks of grey to her chestnut hair and a few new wrinkles around her green eyes, but otherwise she looked exactly the same.

"Hello Mrs. Bledsoe. Is Amy here?"

"Of course dear. She's in her room finishing packing. It's the second door on the left down that hallway." She pointed behind her to the hallway now devoid of family photos and knickknacks.

"Thank you." Chad stepped over the threshold into the nearly empty living room. Blank bookshelves and a couch were all that remained. He wondered where they were moving to and if the move had anything to do with Amy's cryptic call.

The second door on the left was only partially closed, but Chad still knocked before pushing it the rest of the way open. Amy's head popped out of the closet at the slight squeak of the hinges.

"Oh good, you came. Give me a second," she said and a moment later she re-emerged, a stack of clothes slung over one arm. She laid them on the bed and looked up at him. "I guess you can tell we're moving, huh?"

"Yeah, where to?" Chad asked. He

didn't really care, but it seemed impolite not to ask.

"California. My dad got a job out there, so off we go. Not the way I wanted to spend my Senior year, but I guess those are the breaks sometimes, right?" A sad smile crossed her face for an instant before she wiped it away.

At least she would have a Senior year, Chad thought. Kyle never got that chance. "Yeah, life isn't always fair," he said aloud.

She caught the tone in his voice and opened her mouth as if she were going to say something, then thought better of it. Instead, she crossed to the roll top desk, which was devoid of anything except a notebook. Picking it up, she turned back to him and held it out.

"What's this?" he asked, taking the spiral notebook from her.

"It was Kyle's. Our English teacher

made us keep a journal. At first Kyle hated it, but then he got into writing out his feelings and he wrote in it all the time. I guess he left it here one day when we were studying. I found it under my bed." She tucked a strand of dark hair behind her ears and dropped her eyes to the floor. "You need to read it because he wrote about you." Her eyes lifted to Chad's, and in them burned an intensity. "He really looked up to you," she said. "You meant the world to him."

Chad returned her gaze for a moment before opening the notebook. The first few pages held short, choppy paragraphs, and after scanning them, Chad could see this was when Kyle was writing just to fulfill the assignment. But as he turned the pages, the paragraphs grew longer and more detailed. Near the end, the entries were full pages, sometimes more. The last entry in the book was dated only a few days before Kyle's death.

I'm worried about my brother, Chad. He used to be so strong in the faith, but college has changed him. He no longer talks about God much and I haven't seen him pray in ages. Now, all he talks about is girls and I'm afraid he is caving into the pressures of the world. I hope God sends an angel to protect him.

Chad looked up from the page. Kyle had hoped God would send an angel for him? He should have been praying for Kyle's protection, but as he thought back to his Freshman year, he realized Kyle had been right. Chad had started slipping away from God even then. Not like he had after Kyle's death, but with little things - not reading his Bible daily, forgetting to pray, rationalizing physicality in relationships.

"Can I keep this?" he asked Amy. He wanted to read it more in depth and it was a link to Kyle, a side of him he hadn't seen.

Amy nodded. "I can't think of anyone Kyle would want to have it more."

"Thank you," Chad said, clutching the notebook in his hands. He turned to leave, but then paused and faced Amy again. "Kyle cared for you too. I hope you know that."

Tears glistened in her eyes as she nodded. Before her tears could fall and encourage his own, Chad exited her room and the Bledsoe house.

He placed the notebook on the passenger seat beside him before backing the car up and heading toward his parent's house.

CHAPTER 9

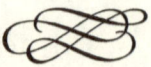

*J*ess stared into the sea of black that was her closet as Emily dressed the next morning.

"What's the matter?" Emily's voice carried over from her side of the room.

"I have nothing to wear. Everything I own is black or holey or"—Jess shrugged —"Not what you wear to church." She didn't know much, but she didn't think miniskirts and crop tops seemed appropriate for church. Tears pricked at the back of her eyes, and she blinked furiously to keep them at bay.

A small, knowing smile spread on Emily's face, and her eyes lit up. She held up a finger, then turned to her closet. After flicking hangers back and forth, she pulled out a blue dress and held it out to Jess. "God doesn't care what you wear, but it is important to feel comfortable. It's not your usual style, but the blue would look great with your eyes, and I think we're close enough in size."

The tears forced their way to the front and blurred Jess's vision. She couldn't remember the last time someone had told her she looked nice when they weren't trying to get her into bed. "Thanks."

As she grabbed the dress, Jess turned her head to wipe the tears away before Emily saw. On one hand, it was just a solid blue piece of fabric, but on the other it was a symbol for so much more.

After slipping on the soft cotton dress, Jess looked in the mirror, stunned at the transformation. The blue did bring out her ocean eyes. Her skin looked pale but smooth, and even her hair appeared less severe.

"See?" Emily asked, coming up behind her. "Beautiful."

Jess nodded, still stunned at how different she looked.

"Oh, they're here," Emily said as her cell phone beeped.

"They?"

"Yeah, Chase and Sarah. Jared needed to go in early today, so Chase and Sarah offered to go with us. Don't worry, they're nice. They're both members of the Students for Life group I'm in." Her eyes dropped back to her phone as she typed back a message.

Jess's nerves crumpled in on each other, and a small voice whispered in her head. Sure, Emily accepted her, but would her friends? She wasn't even sure about this church thing and now she had the added pressure of meeting new people at the same time? Was she doing the right thing? "Maybe I should stay home," Jess said, and the voice agreed. "I don't even have a Bible."

"Don't worry," Emily said, holding out hers. "You can borrow mine. I have it on my phone too."

The small voice rebutted: It wasn't hers; people would know; she could never really fit in. Jess shook her head to stop the negative thoughts and grabbed the Bible. Though it didn't ease all her worries, it seemed to silence the voice. For now, at least. She ran her free hand down the borrowed dress, though no wrinkle was in sight, nodded, and followed Emily out of the room.

A tall guy with sandy blonde hair and

an almost equally tall girl with short spiky blonde hair were waiting for them at the bottom of the stairs.

"Chase, Sarah, I'd like you to meet my roommate Jess," Emily said.

"What's up, Jess?" Chase said with an easy grin.

"So nice to meet you, Jess," Sarah said. Her grey eyes sparkled as she shook Jess's hand. They were the most interesting color she'd ever seen, like the color of fog in the evening. Though her features were sharp, her voice was soft and friendly, and she emitted a calming presence.

"Nice to meet you too," Jess said but her voice lacked its usual confidence. Fears kept popping into her mind. What if the others weren't like Emily and Jared? What if they mocked her for coming? Did she really want to give up a Sunday for this? What if she hated it?

Even as they walked to the parking lot, the questions cycled in Jess's head. Sarah claimed the front seat next to Chase, easing some of her nervousness. Sarah seemed nice, but not knowing her, Jess didn't want to answer a lot of questions or attempt small talk. She swallowed to ease the knots as she climbed in the back seat next to Emily, but they remained resolute.

A few minutes later, they pulled into the church parking lot, and Jess's eyes widened. A large white building loomed in front of them, and the parking lot teemed with cars. "There's so many."

She thought she had only spoken in her head until Emily touched her arm. "It'll be all right. We're all right here with you, and it probably won't seem like so many inside."

Nodding, Jess opened the car door. Other college-aged students meandered in the parking lot. "Is this a University only church?"

"No," Chase laughed, "but they have a great program for high school and college aged students, so a lot come here."

Several young adults stood at the entrance to the church handing out brochures of some kind. Curious, Jess took one, and the group entered the large, open room. Rows of chairs filled it, and a large raised platform occupied most of the front. A piano, drum set, and several guitars sat atop the platform. Three large white screens hung at the front of the room as well, one in the middle and one on each side.

Chase chose a row in the middle aisle and they filed in. Sarah took Chase's left side, Emily his right, and Jess sat on Emily's right, closest to the aisle. As the others chatted quietly, she opened the thin brochure. A listing of activities filled the left side. Groups for men, for women, for teens. It carried into the middle partition.

She couldn't believe how many options were offered. Jess had thought church was just a Sunday thing, but there was something happening nearly every day of the week. A men's and women's ministry on Monday, choir on Tuesday, drama ministry on Wednesday, Teen/college ministry on Thursday, and movie night on Friday. The only day where nothing was listed was Saturday. On the far-right panel, a section for prayer requests filled the top and the bottom held a "Staying Connected" card that you could fill out to give them your information.

As people filled in around them, the hum of conversation grew louder. Jess looked up from the brochure, expecting to see a sea of dresses and suits, but men and women alike sported pants, some even jeans. Maybe Emily had been right about God not caring what people wore.

A few minutes later, several people took the stage. A woman sat down at the piano, a man at the drum set, two men grabbed guitars, and four other men and women picked up microphones Jess hadn't noticed before. The music filled the auditorium, and while the music was not what Jess usually listened to, she enjoyed the sound. She knew none of the words, but her foot tapped along to the rhythm.

When the music ended, the pastor took the stage. As he spoke about Satan using insecurities to pull people away from God, his words hit Jess's heart, and she remembered the voice from earlier trying to convince her not to come. Had that been Satan? She glanced around to see if others were affected. *Is he speaking just to me?* The more he spoke, the more it felt like his words were for her alone, and emotion began bubbling up inside. She wiped her eyes, pretending an eyelash or something was in them and hoping no one else would notice.

When the service ended, people began filing out. Jess followed, but the pastor's words tumbled around in her head. Could it be that she sought male companionship because she was so insecure? Was that Satan attacking her? Even as the group went to lunch, Jess continued to process the words of the preacher.

∼

As Chad sat between his parents and his younger sister in church, a feeling of unease crept in. He felt like a fraud, not having been inside a church in over a year, but his sister had begged him to stay the night when he'd showed up at the house yesterday.

When he'd agreed—only due to his guilt over not seeing her as often as he should—his mother had suggested he attend church with them the next morning. Chad had initially declined, stating his lack of attire as a reason. He hadn't planned on spending the night and therefore hadn't brought a change of clothes with him, but his mother had insisted.

Now as he listened to the pastor's words, he thought back to Kyle's journal. He had read it cover to cover the previous night after dinner. Kyle had been so strong in his faith, and Chad wondered if he had ever been as strong or if he had been merely putting on a show. He certainly couldn't remember thinking the way Kyle had - putting others above himself. Chad had always thought about himself first. Why would God take Kyle who would have been a much better example for others to follow?

"You can always come back to God," the pastor said, his words breaking through Chad's sidetracked thoughts. "He is always waiting for you with open arms. No matter what you've done, God will forgive you if you just ask. Let us pray."

Chad watched as heads around him bowed, but he couldn't follow suit. Not yet. Though he felt something, he wasn't ready to give up his anger yet. God had taken his brother and he needed to know why.

CHAPTER 10

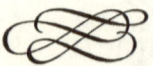

For the first time, Jess dreaded going to class on Monday. It had been over a week since she had spoken with Chad, and after attending church Sunday, she felt more than a little guilty about jumping into bed with him. How was she going to make it through the rest of the semester in his class?

Jess stared at her reflection in the mirror. Though she didn't look that different physically, she felt different. No longer wanting to attract men at every turn, she now opted for longer shirts and shorts that weren't quite as revealing. She wasn't sure if she wanted to keep the shaved part of her hair, but if she parted it down the middle, it was barely noticeable.

Though still new to praying, Jess turned her fears over to God. He would know how to soften this situation with Chad. "Lord, I'm so new I'm not sure if you deal with stuff like this, but I think I messed up. I am not even sure how I feel about Chad now, but I have to see him twice a week, and I'm asking for strength not to fall into temptation again and for peace. Help me get through this semester. Amen."

Jess was glad Emily wasn't in the room as the prayer felt awkward. Did it get easier with time? She'd never been a big fan of public speaking and praying aloud seemed similar, but as stilted as her prayer might have been, a measure of peace blanketed her when her eyes opened.

Chad wasn't in the lecture hall when Jess arrived, and she sighed a breath of relief as she slid into a chair at the back. It was short lived though, as when he walked into the room, her heart thudded in her chest. Why was she still so attracted to him? Was it because they had been intimate or was there something more?

Dropping her gaze to her paper, Jess found she could concentrate on the lecture a little more if she didn't watch him. Still, every once in a while, he would say a word that would trigger a memory in her head and send heat across her cheeks. Would she ever be able to get him out of her head?

"Hey, I saw you at Indiana Avenue Baptist yesterday, right?"

The voice startled her, and Jess looked up in surprise at the guy in front of her.

With her focus on avoiding Chad's gaze as she gathered her books together, she hadn't noticed this stranger approach as the rest of the students filed out.

"Uh, yeah," she responded as she stood and slung the backpack over her shoulder. "It was my first week."

"I wondered," he said with a smile. "I didn't think I had seen you there before. I'm Randall, by the way."

As Jess took his hand, her gaze wandered down front to find Chad staring at them. Their eyes locked for a moment before he shoved the rest of his papers in his satchel and exited the side door. A part of her wanted to run after him, but the more rational part realized it was better this way. Perhaps Randall was her answer to prayer as a way to avoid temptation.

"Uh, Jess," she said, focusing her attention back on the dude in front of her. "I'm Jess."

"So, did you like it?" he asked as they walked out of the row towards the door.

"Yeah, I did," Jess said. "I'm new to church but it was nice there, and my roommate Emily Peters attends there."

His eyes lit up. "Oh yeah, I know Emily. She played on the church softball team last spring."

"The church has a softball team?" Jess asked as the two stepped into the sunshine.

"Yep, and a volleyball team during the winter. Can you serve?"

"I don't know," she said with a laugh. The truth was, she'd never given sports a chance in high school. She had wanted to avoid the camaraderie that generally went along with team sports as she had wanted no one finding out about her home life. Plus, she had never known when her mother would be sober and allow her to attend games or be drunk and forbid it.

He raised his eyebrow at the response and Jess shook her head. "It's a long story," she said. "Suffice to say, I didn't play any sports in high school, so I have no idea if I'm good at any of them."

"Well, you should definitely try out this year then," he said. "We have a lot of fun."

"I'll think about it," she agreed. "I'm this way." Jess pointed to the right where the math building lay.

Disappointment filled his brown eyes. "Oh, I'm this way." He pointed to the left. "Well, it was nice to see you again, Jess, and I guess I'll see you Wednesday, right?"

"I'll be there," she said and returned his wave before he walked away. As she continued to the math building, she found herself wondering if Randall's interest had been purely platonic or if he were interested in her. Having never had a "normal" relationship, Jess found she had no idea how it was supposed to work. Her history had always been find a man, hook up, repeat. She would have to ask Emily how to navigate these new, unfamiliar waters.

~

A feeling of jealousy welled up in Chad's stomach as he watched the boy interact with Jess. He shouldn't be jealous as he hadn't called her in a week. Plus, if she were willing to jump into bed with him, she had probably already found someone to take his place, but the feeling remained.

Maybe he should have answered her question. What did he care if she knew his favorite food was Chicken Alfredo? The truth was - he didn't. He had been scared. Scared that she wanted a relationship that he wasn't ready for. Was he? Frustrated, he shoved his papers in the satchel and stormed out the side door. A cigarette, that's what he needed.

As the door closed behind him with a soft click, he dropped his satchel and leaned against the brick wall. He snaked a cigarette and his lighter out of his pocket and flicked the flame on. The calming effect was nearly immediate.

What was wrong with him? He didn't need to be developing feelings for some girl. But Jess wasn't just some girl. She intrigued him in a way no woman had in years, and he didn't even know why. What he did know was that she occupied his thoughts a lot, more than he wanted, but falling for her meant opening up a side of himself he had closed off with Kyle's death.

Ever since Amy's call, Chad's life had been in a tailspin and going home had only made it worse. The journal from

Kyle, seeing his sister, and attending church had all stirred up feelings and emotions he thought he had long ago buried.

The cigarette burned to a nub, stinging his fingers. With a curse, he dropped it to the ground and smashed it into the dirt with his toe. He needed answers before he could really process his feelings.

CHAPTER 11

*A*voiding Chad grew a little easier after that. Though he often popped into Jess's head, she found ways to fill her time to avoid focusing on him. Her job kept her busy for one, and on Friday nights, she attended the Bible Study with Emily. The roommates had also started a Saturday movie night to keep them both out of trouble. Plus, Randall started sitting next to her in class and walking her out each day.

"I ought to like him, right?" Jess asked

Emily as she pulled the popcorn bag from the microwave and opened it. The sweet buttery smell of the popcorn filled the air as a cloud of steam billowed from the bag. Careful not to burn her fingers, Jess tilted the bag until the oily, yellow kernels filled the metallic bowl. Though she loved microwaved popcorn, she had never liked eating it directly out of the bag due to the residue it left on her hand. Plus, it was harder to share that way.

"You want my honest opinion?"

"Of course."

"Well, just because he's nice and a Christian doesn't mean you'll be attracted to him," Emily said as she popped the DVD in the player. Jess had rented When Love Returns, the small town love story from the Redbox at the Student Union before leaving work for the day. "If we were attracted to every Christian man, that would be a mess. I mean if that were the case, I'd be attracted to Jared and Chase and…"

"You mean you aren't?" Jess teased her. "I've seen the way you look at Jared."

"No way," she said with an adamant shake of her head. "Jared and I are just friends. We tried dating last year, but it didn't work out. Besides, he likes this new girl, Amanda. Anyway, it's not about liking Randall exactly; it's about finding a guy with those qualities. Someone of faith who loves the Lord."

Jess joined Emily on the bed and placed the bowl between them. "I guess you're right. I just feel bad. Like I should be attracted to him, but honestly… I can't get Chad out of my head."

"Is that the guy I walked in on?" Emily asked with a raised eyebrow.

"Yes," Jess said slowly and then continued in a hurry before Emily could interrupt, "I know it's wrong - that he's wrong for me, but thoughts of him just keep flying in, even when I don't want them there."

"Have you tried praying about it?" Emily asked.

"All the time," Jess said with a sigh. "It's probably selfish, but I was really hoping God would make me magically forget how attracted to him I was. It hasn't happened yet."

Emily popped a kernel in her mouth and chewed slowly. "Well, have you tried praying for him?"

"What?"

"Pray for him," she said. "He is in your life for a reason. He may not be healthy for you right now, but maybe God's plan was to have you be a seed in his journey to redemption. I also think you should avoid relationships for a bit anyway. Get to know yourself and what you really want before trying to blend your life with someone else's."

As the movie began, Jess leaned back against the wall and pondered Emily's words. She was right that Jess needed to find herself, but she didn't understand how she could be a seed for anyone's redemption. There was still so much in her past she was ashamed of.

~

"*T*hank you for meeting me," Chad said as he sat across from the chaplain. Not being a church goer, Chad was unfamiliar with the pastors in the area, but he knew the campus had a chaplain on staff.

"Of course," the man said. He was older, with salt and pepper hair and laugh lines around his eyes. "What can I do for you?"

"I have some questions," Chad said. "About God."

"Well, that is my specialty," the man said with a smile, "but I don't claim to know everything. Only God does that. Still, I'll be happy to answer what I can."

"Why does God allow suffering?" Chad asked.

"Ah," the chaplain said, "that is a common question. The truth is that we don't know the answer. God allows free will and because there is sin in the world, often that free will leads to suffering for others."

"But why would he take someone good? See, my brother had a heart for God unlike me. He was a true believer. So why would God take him instead of me?"

"Oh, son, I'm sorry you lost your brother, but God doesn't work like that. Your brother was affected by someone else's free will, and sometimes that means bad things happen to good people. But, it sounds like your brother was prepared to meet God."

"But couldn't God have stopped it? Couldn't he just have kept my brother from getting killed?" Chad pushed.

The chaplain sat back in his brown leather chair. "I suppose he could have, but let me ask you this - if your brother were still alive, would you be here in my office?"

"What do you mean?" Chad asked.

"You said your brother was a true believer. I take that to mean you weren't, that you acted as if you were, but you weren't really, am I right?"

Chad shrugged, not liking where this was going all of a sudden. "I guess. I mean I attended church, but I wasn't dedicated like Kyle was."

"So, am I safe in assuming if your brother was still alive that you would still be on that path? Talking the talk but not walking the walk?"

"Are you saying my actions got my brother killed?"

"Not at all, but I am saying that we don't know God's plan. We only see the lower story, what's happening down here. But God sees a much larger plan from his viewpoint."

Chad sat back and thought about the chaplain's words. Could it be that his anger had been misplaced?

As if reading his mind, the chaplain leaned forward again and said, "You know God understands when we are angry with him. It doesn't make Him love us any less, and He is still waiting to accept us with open arms when we are ready to come home."

Chad nodded as he thanked the chaplain and headed out of the office. Kyle's last few journal entries had been about wishing Chad would renew his relationship with Jesus. Could he do that? Could he get over his anger at God and be the man that his brother had hoped he would become? And what about his lifestyle, would that have to change too? And where did Jess fit into all of this? Chad had come to the chaplain for answers, but he was leaving with a lot of questions too.

CHAPTER 12

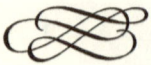

The next morning, Jess awoke with a start. Something was wrong, but she couldn't put a finger on it. It was dark for one thing. As she didn't have classes until the afternoon, she rarely woke before the sun, but that wasn't the main issue. Today was Sunday and there were no classes anyway.

As Jess tried to focus on what had woken her up, her stomach seized, and she suddenly knew. Throwing back the covers, she vaulted out of bed and rushed to the sink. She would never make it to the bathroom down the hall in time. This would have to do. With a final clench, her stomach heaved its contents into the sink.

When the sickness subsided, Jess rinsed the sink and her mouth out and then splashed cool water on her face.

"Jess, are you okay?" Emily mumbled from her side of the room. "What time is it?"

"Early," Jess answered. "Go back to sleep. It must have been something I ate. I'll be fine." But as she walked back to her bed, she wondered if that were true. With a cast iron stomach, Jess couldn't remember the last time any food had made her sick.

The sunlight peeked in the next time Jess opened her eyes. Emily still slept on the opposite side of the room. Saturdays and Sundays were the only days Emily could sleep in, though to her that meant eight am and not Jess's idea of nearly noon. The room lay quiet aside from her rhythmic breathing. Jess paused for a moment, testing her stomach, but it appeared to have settled.

She pushed back the covers before sitting up slowly and planting her feet on the floor. So far so good, but as she stood, her stomach clenched again, and she hurried to the sink a second time. What was wrong with her? She hadn't thrown up this much since...

Her eyes widened, and she raced back to her bed, grabbing the backpack from the floor and pawing through it for her birth control pills. Her mother had put her on them at sixteen when she found out about the miscarriage. Jess suffered through her mother's lecture on safe sex, but couldn't find the courage at the time to tell her the baby was Jim's. After all, she hadn't believed Jess when she'd told her mother he touched her, why would she have believed that? And the pill opened the door to other men after that, ones Jess could choose to help her forget her stepfather, if only for a time.

Jess's fingers grasped the package, and she pulled it out, flipping over the cover. All the pills had been taken, no gap existed in the line. A sigh of relief escaped her lips. What would she have done if she were pregnant? So as not to forget, she popped out the pill for today and froze. Today's pill was labeled Saturday, but it was Sunday morning. Had she skipped it yesterday? No, she remembered taking the pill shortly after waking up yesterday. Friday, then?

With a sinking feeling, Jess plopped down onto the bed as she realized she had no idea when she'd missed a pill. This pack or last? In fact, she couldn't even remember if she'd had her period with the last pack. Typically regular like clockwork and light enough that she barely noticed it, she had stopped charting her period and just known it would hit when the pills changed color. Unfortunately, now she couldn't place having one in the last month which meant there was a very real chance her "sickness" was morning sickness.

Across the room, Emily stirred and stretched in her bed. "You feeling better?" she asked, her voice still fuzzy with sleep.

Jess couldn't tell her. She wanted to, but she couldn't. The need to process the situation seemed more important. "Um, not so much," Jess said. "I think I'll have to skip church today. I don't want to get anyone else sick."

"That bad, huh?" She tugged a hand through the tangled blonde mess on her head.

"Yeah, I think I'm going to try to

sleep this off, whatever it is." She hated lying. The first thing she planned to do when Emily left was head to the campus drugstore for a pregnancy test. Hopefully they would be open on Sundays.

"Do you want me to get anything for you while I'm out?" she asked as she gathered up her shower items.

"No, I'm sure it will go away on its own." Or with some help, she thought.

~

E had looked at his reflection in the mirror and wondered again what he was doing. Attending church two weeks in a row was a foreign concept to him, but he couldn't shake the sensation he needed to be there. He had no idea where *there* was though. Lubbock was one of the most churched cities in Texas. You could barely go three blocks without running into one.

After asking around, he found Indiana Avenue promoted a strong college program and that many students from the University attended there, so he had picked that as his first choice to try. If he didn't find what he needed there, he would try another church the next week. The only problem was Chad didn't know what he needed or what he was looking for, but he felt sure he would know it when he found it.

The parking lot teemed with college aged students when he arrived. He maneuvered the Harley into a spot and turned off the key.

Chad joined the throng of people funneling into the entrance and found himself in a large foyer. Ahead he could see the open doors of the sanctuary and he continued that direction, finding an empty seat near the back. He stowed his helmet under the chair and then perused the brochure he had been handed at the door.

When the music started, he glanced up and realized the room had filled up around him. Empty seats remained though not many. Most of the surrounding people stood as they sang. Self-consciously, he rose though he didn't know the words to a few of the songs.

Relief flooded Chad when the pastor took the stage and the congregation sat. However, that relief was short-lived as the pastor began to speak on being different from the world.

"You see, Jesus called us to be in the world but separate from it. However, that has gotten much harder with technology. TV and movies tell us that smoking, drinking, cursing, cheating, and intimacy outside of marriage are not only okay but the norm. And the media assaults us with the mantra that if it feels good, we should do it, that God would want us to be happy. But the truth is, God wants us to be holy.

"Now some of you may ask yourselves, 'But doesn't God forgive our sins if we ask?' The answer is He does, but mercy and grace were never meant to be an excuse to sin. It was to save us with the expectation we would then turn away from our sin. Remember he told the woman at the well to 'go and sin no more.' He expects the same from us, and it's hard, but if we love Christ, we should want to be different."

He paused and scanned the crowd. "Some of you may be wondering what to do now because you have already started down a path created by the world and not by God. The answer is to repent, to turn away from your sin, and to follow Jesus."

As the preacher ended the sermon with prayer, Chad felt the weight of his sins bearing down on him. He had been doing nearly everything the preacher spoke on. Chad knew what he needed to do, but he wasn't ready yet. Something held him back from fully re-committing his life to Jesus, and as he walked outside the building and mounted his motorcycle again, the pastor's words began to fade and with them the sense of urgency.

~

*J*ess stared at the small plastic stick. Though she had been nearly positive she was pregnant, seeing the two blue lines confirming it still elicited a shock. What was she going to do now? She hadn't even spoken to Chad in weeks; she had little money and no way to raise a baby. As much as she didn't want to think about it, abortion seemed like the best option. It would allow her to have the fresh start she was looking for and she wouldn't have to tell Emily…

No. Correction. She could never tell Emily. Emily would not understand, but Emily was not in her shoes.

The sound of a key in the door snapped Jess back to reality, and she shoved the stick under some clothes on her bed mere seconds before Emily entered the room.

"Hey, Jess, are you feeling any better?"

"A little," Jess said which wasn't a total lie. She had been able to keep down food the last hour. Still, guilt crept in for not telling Emily the whole truth. "How was church?"

"Really good. The pastor spoke on not following what the world says and standing strong in faith."

"It sounds like a good one," Jess said. "I'm sorry I missed it." Inside though, Jess was glad she'd missed it. She felt guilty enough about her plan to have an abortion. Listening to the pastor would have probably made it worse. She just needed to take care of it this week and then she could repent and really focus on doing God's will.

CHAPTER 13

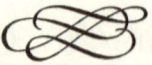

*J*ess slipped out of bed as quietly as possible. She would have to come up with some excuse to explain to Emily where she'd gone when she returned, but she had to get this taken care of before she lost her nerve.

Last night, she'd researched abortion clinics on her phone and found the closest one lay in Fort Worth - six hours away. Unfortunately, Jess didn't have a car, so she also looked into buses. The earliest one left at six am, so she'd set the alarm for five and turned it to the quietest setting she dared. She wasn't sure if the alarm had woken her, or if she'd never gone to sleep the night before.

Jess grabbed her toothbrush, toothpaste, wallet, jacket, and shoes and slipped out of the room. Having slept in the clothes she planned to wear today to cut down on the chances of waking Emily, she now padded silently to the bathroom to brush her teeth and pull on her shoes.

Five minutes later, Jess pushed open the dorm doors and trekked across the dark campus to the bus stop. The street lamps cast an eerie glow across the grass as the sun was not yet out, and a sense of relief filled Jess when the small bus shelter came into view. She huddled in the corner, pulling her knees to her chest to combat the cold and waited for the bus to arrive.

~

*C*had thought about what he would say to Jess as he crossed the campus. He'd spent the previous evening thinking about Kyle and his own life. Though not sure he was ready to commit - either to Jesus or to a relationship - he needed to apologize to Jess for his behavior. Plus, he wanted to see if she still wanted to hang out, so they could get to know each other this time.

As he neared the Psychology building, a female figure near the side door caught his eye. Could it be Jess waiting for him? Was she having second thoughts as well? But when the girl turned, he realized it was not Jess.

His heart sank as the distance closed, and he realized the girl was Jess's uptight roommate.

"Have you seen her?" the girl asked when he was within ear shot.

"Not yet, but class is about to start. She should be here soon."

"Can I come in and wait for her?" Worry lines creased the girl's pretty face.

"Why? What's wrong?" Chad asked as a sinking sensation filled his stomach.

"I don't know." The girl tucked a strand of hair behind her ears. "Maybe nothing, but she was gone this morning when I got up. She's never gone. She sleeps until noon. And yesterday she was sick, throwing up, and she skipped church. I'm just worried about her."

"Maybe she was still sick this morning and she left early so she wouldn't wake you," Chad offered, but in his heart, he didn't think that was the case, and now a seed of worry joined the sinking sensation, creating a churning nauseous feeling.

"Can I just check?" she continued. "I'll leave if she's not there, but will you tell her to call me if she shows up after I'm gone?"

"Sure, yeah. Come on," Chad said, opening the door for her. The two scanned the crowd, but Jess was nowhere to be seen. Chad dug a paper and pen out of his satchel, scrawled his number on the paper, and handed it to the girl. "Text me, so I have your number, and I'll text back whether or not she shows up."

"Thank you." The girl took the paper from him, scanned the crowd with worried eyes one last time, and then turned and exited the room.

Chad took out his supplies for class, but his mind was elsewhere. Where was Jess? And was she okay? It would be a long hour.

~

*J*ess looked at Emily's number flashing across her caller ID and sighed. Emily had been calling every hour since seven am. She should have known Emily would worry about her. Maybe she should have left a note or maybe she could text and at least let Emily know she was ok. But what would she say?

"Boy troubles?"

Jess looked up at the woman next to her who had spoken. Kind brown eyes stared back at her from a weathered and wrinkled face. The woman had to be in her seventies.

"No, my roommate," Jess said. "I left without telling her this morning and she's worried about me."

"Ah," the woman said with a knowing nod. "Why don't you just tell her where you're at?"

"I…" Jess didn't know. Emily couldn't stop her now even if she told her, but the truth was Jess never wanted Emily to know what she was doing, and she had no lie concocted yet.

"It's the secrets that hurt us the most," the woman said, and sadness clouded her eyes. "I remember my Maggie used to be so carefree until her secrets festered inside her. Then she grew distant and she stopped coming around."

"What happened to her?" The words slipped out of Jess's mouth. She didn't want to engage this woman in conversation, but she wanted to know.

"She took her own life a year ago. In her suicide note, she wrote how she couldn't handle the guilt of what she'd done, and she hoped God would forgive her for taking another's life."

Jess's hand flew to her mouth. "She killed someone?"

"A teenage girl," the woman said. "She was driving drunk and ran a red light. She served over a year in prison, but she sobered up while she was inside. I wish she had told me when she got out how she was feeling. I know what she did was wrong, but every life is precious to God."

A new wave of guilt washed over Jess and she wished she had never conversed with the elderly woman. As her phone buzzed again, Jess reached for the power button, but her eyes landed on the caller ID screen and she paused. The number flashing this time was not Emily's but Chad's. Why was he calling her?

Jess let the call go to voicemail and then listened to the message. "Jess? It's Chad. Your roommate came looking for you. She's worried about you and frankly so am I. Where are you? At least let us know you're okay, please?"

The tone in his voice was the last straw. Tears spilled out of Jess's eyes and coursed down her cheek. What was she doing? She couldn't have an abortion; she hadn't even told Chad she was pregnant.

"Are you all right, dear?" the woman asked.

Jess shook her head. "I'm not, but as soon as I can get off this bus I will be. Thank you for sharing your story with me. I.... I'm pregnant and I was headed to Fort Worth to have an abortion, but your story and that call.... That was the baby's father. He doesn't even know…"

"Are you a believer, my dear?" the woman asked with tears in her eyes.

"I'm almost ashamed to say I am after what I was considering," Jess said, "but I'm very new to this."

"My daughter was a believer too when she had her accident," the woman said. "I think it's what made her guilt even worse. I prayed often for her to come back to me and when she didn't, I was angry for a time at God. But then He showed me that good things can come out of tragedies, and so I began to pray that Maggie's story would help others. He answered my prayers today."

At that, more tears escaped Jess's eyes and the two women hugged and prayed together before the bus stopped and Jess deboarded to switch busses for one headed back to Lubbock. As she waited for the bus that would take her back, she sent a text to Emily letting her know she was okay and one to Chad asking him to come by her dorm that evening. She knew she would have to tell them what she had almost done, but it needed to be in person and not over the phone.

*R*elief flooded Chad at Jess's message. She was okay. That was the main thing, but where had she been and what did she have to tell him? Had she found someone else? Would he be okay if she had? The more he thought about it, the clearer the answer became. No, he would not be okay. His worry over her today solidified the feelings he had been denying. He cared for her, and regardless of what she told him tonight, he would tell her how he felt.

CHAPTER 14

*J*ess gathered her courage in the hallway before opening the door. As soon as Jess crossed the doorjamb, Emily bounded across the room and engulfed her in a hug.

"Where were you? Why didn't you leave me a note? Or text me you were okay? I was so worried." The words streamed out of Emily's mouth with a rapid-fire intensity.

"I'm sorry," Jess said. Was she really going to tell Emily? What if Emily hated her afterwards? What if she no longer wanted to be friends? Jess shook her head to clear the thoughts. Emily wouldn't do that. "I need to talk to you, but you should sit down."

Emily followed Jess's lead and sat down on her bed, her hands clasped in her lap.

Jess opened her mouth to speak, but then decided evidence would be more powerful. She crossed to her dresser and retrieved the white stick from under the clothes where she had stashed it at her first opportunity.

Emily's eyes widened as she realized what lay in Jess's hand, and her mouth dropped open in a perfect "o" shape. "Oh, Jess, I'm so sorry, but we'll figure something out. We have several places you can contact for information on adoption or financial assistance if you decide you want to raise the baby." Horror dawned on Emily's face. "Or did you…."

Tears flooded Jess's eyes, blurring the room around her. She sank onto the bed next to Emily. "I didn't, but I was on my way, Emily. I knew it was wrong, which is why I didn't tell you, but I have nothing. I thought it would be easier if…"

"Don't even consider it," Emily said. "That could be me. That was going to be my fate until God stepped in. He has a plan for you too, and it does not include getting rid of this child."

"I was so worried you would hate me," Jess said. "I've messed up so much."

"Jess, I could never hate you. You're my sister in Christ, and no matter how much you mess up, I will be there, and Jesus will be there for you." Her eyes widened. "Does Chad know?"

Jess shook her head. "I asked him to

meet me here at seven, so I could tell him."

"Jess, it's six forty-five," Emily said.

"Oh, crap," Jess said, jumping up from the bed. "What do I say to him?" She paced back and forth in the room. It was a good thing the floor was already old because Jess felt like she would have worn a crevice in a new carpet.

"The truth," Emily replied. "Whether he wants to be a part of it or not, he deserves to know he has a son or daughter coming. I'll step out to give you privacy, but I'll be right downstairs if you need me."

Jess nodded, but her heart continued to pound a beat in her head. She'd practiced what she would tell him on the bus ride home, but now that the time was nearly here, her stomach twisted in knots. Taking a deep breath, Jess smoothed her shirt and sat on the bed, tapping her fingers on the mattress. Her leg jiggled back and forth of its own accord.

"It will be okay," Emily said from across the room.

Jess envied her calm demeanor. Of course, she wasn't the one carrying the baby, but she somehow thought even if Emily was that she would be calm.

A knock sounded at the door, and Jess's heart jumped. Emily flashed a thumb-up as she walked to the door. Chad, dark and sexy, stood on the other side in a black leather jacket and jeans. At the sight of him, Jess's heart sped up. He still affected her, and though she saw him twice a week in class, seeing him out of class and in her doorway felt different.

"I'll just let you two have some time," Emily said, squeezing past Chad.

As Chad stepped into the room and

closed the door behind him, Jess felt her old nature start to kick in. The words could wait. She could pull him onto the bed and lose herself in his arms. After all, she was already pregnant, so there was no fear of that. No, that was no longer her life. She would stand up to temptation.

"Jess," he said, closing the distance between them.

She placed her fingers on his lips, trying to ignore the tremor of emotion that shot through her. "Wait, let me go first before I lose my nerve."

Chad nodded and reached for her hand, but the smell of his cologne was intoxicating. Jess had to distance herself. She crossed to the window, gathering her thoughts, before turning to face him. "Um, so okay you remember when we..."—she looked down at her hands and then at her bed, unable to verbalize the act, but he understood and nodded, prodding her to continue. "Well, I'm pregnant."

His eyes widened. His mouth opened and closed; then opened again. He ran his hand across his stubbled chin. "Are you sure? I mean it's been so long. We were together the last time over a month ago."

Jess's face flamed. "I know, but I hadn't realized I was late until I started getting sick. I took a test this weekend, and I've only been with you."

"Wow, okay um." His hands trailed down his denim-clad thighs before he turned his blue eyes on her—oh, those eyes. "What do you want to do?"

"I'm going to have the baby," she said. "I thought I wanted an abortion which is where I was today - on the way to the nearest clinic, but your call, an old woman, and God changed my mind."

She chuckled at his puzzled expression. "It's a long story, but I'm not asking anything from you. I'll put the baby up for adoption."

He nodded, blinking a few times. Then his hand again grazed his chin. The simple nervous gesture sent her heart racing. What was wrong with her?

"No."

"No?" she asked.

"Well, I'm not sure. Look, Jess, I don't know if I'm ready to be a father. I didn't even think I wanted a relationship, but I can't stop thinking about you. I've been making some changes in my life too, and I'm sorry for the way I treated you the last time we were together. It was selfish and wrong, but I was pushing you away because of fear. That's a story for another day. However, after Emily came looking for you today and I didn't know what had happened to you, I couldn't deny I had feelings any longer. I want us to be together, the right way this time. Let's get to know each other and then we can decide about the baby."

Jess's head dropped forward, and her eyes widened. Was he for real? She had thought he would push her to have an abortion or run screaming at the very least, but here he was telling her he had feelings for her. "I don't know, Chad," she managed to stutter. "I mean I'm not the same person. Jesus is a part of my life now, and I'm trying to live the way He wants me. And you," she stepped back as he approached her, but there was nowhere else to go - she was backed up against the window. "You are like playing with fire. I'm not sure I could date you and behave."

The last words came out little more

than a whisper as his hand circled her neck and tangled in her hair.

"I'd like to try," he said in a husky voice before claiming her lips with his own.

~

As Chad left Jess's room later, fear and elation cycled through his veins. Kissing her had been amazing - he had definitely missed it - but his desire for her hadn't changed, and it had been hard to stop himself this time. So hard! The bed was right there, and her scent had driven him crazy. But he had refrained. However, he knew more time spent together would mean more temptation to face. He would have to give that to God.

It was funny how the thought of losing someone made everything so clear. Not only had he decided he wanted a relationship with Jess when he'd heard she was missing, but he had wanted to talk to God then too. As he crossed the campus, he wished Kyle was still here to talk to. He might have been younger, but from his journal he appeared to have his life more together than Chad did.

When he got back to his room, Chad pulled Kyle's journal out of his desk drawer and sat down to read it again. His brother's words had been so full of wisdom, and as he read over Kyle's entries of dealing with his own temptation around Amy, Chad knew what he had to do.

"Jesus? I know I wandered and thought I could do things my own way, but I realize I need you. Forgive me for sinning and help me to follow your ways now. Give me the strength to resist the physical temptation and show me how to be a man of God."

As he finished the prayer, Chad looked back down at the journal. At the bottom of the entry, Kyle had penned: Pray Unceasingly. *Okay, God,* Chad thought. *I'll pray and trust that you'll show me the way.*

CHAPTER 15

*J*ess stood outside the brick building trying to calm her heart. A gentle touch at her elbow caused her to turn to Emily who flashed an encouraging smile. "Thanks for coming with me."

"Of course," Emily said and gestured to the door.

Jess knew she had to go in, but her feet felt encased in cement, and her arm stuck like Velcro to her side. Taking this step would change her life forever, and she wasn't sure she was ready.

Emily held out her hand, and Jess managed to move her arm enough to grasp it. Emily pulled open the door with one hand and Jess forward with the other. Though slow, Jess's feet stumbled forward, and she stepped onto the smooth floor.

The foyer broke into several halls, and a large curved desk sat in the middle manned by two women. An ocean of beige carpet separated the girls from the desk, but Emily plowed forward, dragging Jess along.

"Can I help you?" the woman to the left asked at their approach.

Jess cleared her throat, hoping her voice would work better than her feet had so far. "Yes, I'm pregnant, and I wanted to speak to someone about help."

"Absolutely, you can have a seat over

there"—she pointed to the waiting area just to the side—"and we'll call you back as soon as we can. Also, I need you to fill out this paperwork." She handed over a metal clipboard with several sheets of white paper attached, which Jess grasped tightly as she turned to the chairs.

The chairs, upholstered in a blue fabric, formed two rows of ten chairs each. She plopped down in one of the empty ones on the first row, and Emily sat next to her. Clicking the back of the pen, Jess began to fill in the paperwork. Name, address, date of last period. It seemed to be a standard medical history form, and the monotonous scratching of the pen eased her nerves. After finishing the first side, she flipped it over. Questions of a different sort filled this side.

Has anyone been adopted in your family? What kind of adoption would you

like to have? *Kind? There are different kinds?*
The questions continued, and Jess
answered them the best she could. Yes,
she would need help with medical care.
No, she didn't have family close by. Yes,
the father knew. No, he wouldn't fight the
adoption. Or, at least she thought he
wouldn't. They hadn't really discussed it
much after the kiss.

"Tara, it's so good to see you," Emily
said. Jess looked up from the paperwork as
Emily rose to greet a blonde girl about
their age. The girl wore a loose fitting blue
shirt and black pants. "I didn't realize this
was where you worked."

"Yep, ever since the day we spoke at
the Students for Life office. I started
answering phones, but I recently got a
promotion, so now I get to start the
process."

"That's so amazing."

"Are you here with Jess Peterson?"

Tara asked Emily, before glancing Jess's direction.

"Yes, she's my roommate," Emily said, then turned and made introductions.

"Nice to meet you Jess. If you'll follow me, we can talk in a more private room."

Jess stood, still grasping the clipboard like a flotation device in choppy water and followed Tara and Emily down a long grey hallway and into a tiny grey room. A small desk crowded one corner of the office. Two blue chairs, like the ones in the waiting area, sat across from the desk. Books filled a small bookshelf in the other corner, and pictures of parents holding a baby lined the wall behind the desk. Though packed full, the room felt cozy.

"Did you unite all those families?" Emily asked, pointing to the wall as they sat down.

Tara smiled, "No, I inherited this office and the pictures, but these three are mine. Or at least partially mine. I answered the phones on the day they called and got them to come in." She pointed to the bottom three pictures.

"So, how does this work?" Jess asked, interrupting. She hadn't meant for the words to sound rude, but her nerves were on edge. She was here to give her baby away and that was tough to deal with.

Tara recovered nicely and even flashed a smile. "Well, we'll fill out a list of what you'd like in adoptive parents. We'll get the paperwork started for the financial aspect, and you can look through the binder today if you'd like."

"Binder?" Emily asked.

Tara pulled a large black binder to the center of the desk. "This is a listing of all the couples waiting to adopt in the near area. You can read all about them, see pictures, and decide if you like any of them. I suggest you pick five to six couples you like and then narrow it down from there. Of course, you can meet any of the couples you'd like as well." With a swipe of the mouse, Tara brought the computer screen to life. "Okay, let's get the basic questions out of the way. Do you care if the couple has other children?"

Jess's eyes were glued to the binder. Were the people who would adopt her baby in there?

"Jess," Emily poked her, and Jess's head jerked up.

"I'm sorry, what was the question?"

"Do you care if the couple has other children?" Tara repeated patiently.

"No, I don't think it would matter."

"Okay, religion? Do you want them to be religious and do you have any specific religion?"

"Just Christian is fine, but yes, that's high on my list." Though still learning about God herself, Jess wanted the baby to be in a loving, Christian home like Emily had grown up in.

Tara clicked a few keys and continued to rattle off questions. There was so much involved in the process, and Jess wanted to finish so she could look through the binder. Finally, the questions were complete.

"Do you have any questions for me?" Tara asked.

"Does the binder contain pictures of the couples?" Jess's fingers itched to open the cover and devour the pages.

"Of course." Tara turned the binder around. "This was my favorite part when I decided on adoption. Just a few more months to go." She patted her belly, and Jess did a double-take. The idea that she was like Jess, young and unmarried, gave Jess hope that things would work out for her.

"How is it going?" Emily asked.

As Tara answered, Jess's attention returned to the book. She touched the cover, suddenly unsure. What if none of the people called out to her? Swallowing her apprehension, she flipped open the cover.

A nice-looking man and woman stared up at her. Beneath the picture, a bio of the couple and what they were looking for filled the page. Jess skimmed it before turning the page. Another couple, blonde. Another, brunette. The couples seemed so similar, and there were so many of them. How would she ever decide?

As Jess continued to flip through the pages, she found it easier to eliminate couples than to pick couples. She didn't want the parents to smoke; she wanted a two parent household; some education was a must, but by the time she reached the end of the binder, Jess still wasn't sure.

"Did you find a few you liked?" Tara asked.

Jess bit her lip and shook her head. "I don't know. Do I have to decide right now?"

"Of course not," Tara said with an encouraging smile. "You can think about it and come back and look through the binder whenever you'd like or if you have a list of items you know are necessities or deal breakers, I can run it through the system and send you potential candidates."

"Okay," Jess said. "What about the father? Does he have a say? Should I be asking him?"

Tara's forehead furrowed, and she looked from Emily to Jess. "Is he in the picture? I only ask because usually they aren't, so I just assumed."

"Um, he's not, I guess. I mean we're together, I think, but he said he wasn't ready to raise a baby. I simply wondered if he had a legal say in any of this."

"Only if he decides to fight the adoption," Tara said. "Otherwise, it's pretty much your decision as long as he signs the papers. Of course, if you are together, you're welcome to bring him in and have him look with you. Maybe his perspective will help you decide."

Jess nodded, trying to process all the information. Suddenly, she was no longer sure of anything. "Can I take time to think about it?"

"Absolutely," Tara said. "We have the process started which is the important thing. You can come make changes whenever you'd like. We are here to help you."

"It was good to see you again," Emily said to Tara as the girls stood to leave. "I'm so glad things seem to be working out for you."

As the two walked out of the office, Jess couldn't help but wonder if things would work out for her.

~

*C*had stared at the bouquet of red roses in his hands and smiled. He had no idea if Jess even liked flowers, but what woman didn't like roses? And if she hated them, then perhaps she would at least appreciate the gesture.

He rapped gently on her door and waited for it to swing open.

"Oh, Chad, they're beautiful," Jess said as the door opened, and her eyes landed on the flowers. "But, I have no place to put them." Her brow furrowed as she turned to survey the room.

"Don't worry, I'll see what I can find," Jess's roommate said as she rose from her bed and took the flowers from Jess. Chad would have to find out her name again.

"So, where are we going?" Jess asked as she took his arm.

"You'll see." Chad led the way to his motorcycle parked downstairs and handed her the spare helmet. When he was sure Jess was secure behind him, he fired up the bike and headed toward his favorite park.

As the air was cooling the closer it got to winter, Chad had packed a few blankets along with the food in his saddlebags and told Jess to wear a coat. Her jacket looked old and worn though, and he made a mental note to purchase her a nice leather one soon, especially if she would be riding with him more often.

"So, you once asked me what my favorite food was," he said after turning off the engine and removing his helmet. "I thought instead of just telling you, I would share it with you." He swung off the bike and helped her down before grabbing the supplies from the saddlebags.

"I can't believe you remember that," she said with a soft smile. "I thought as fast as you got out of there that you wouldn't remember my silly question."

He returned her smile. "I may have behaved badly, but it didn't mean I wasn't listening. Now, I am not a great cook, so I have to admit that I got this to go. I hope it's still warm enough."

"I'm sure it will be fine."

Chad led the way to a large tree that still had some of its leaves and spread the blanket out underneath. Then he opened the boxes he had picked up from Carino's and handed one to Jess. "Chicken Alfredo. That's my favorite food. Along with French Bread and pretty much anything Italian."

"I love Italian too," Jess said with a smile.

Chad liked seeing that smile on her face and he decided he would do his best to keep it there.

CHAPTER 16

The next Psychology class was hard to sit through. Chad's eyes kept wandering to Jess's, and she felt like everyone in the class could tell they shared a secret. As the class ended, Chad kept glancing her direction as he packed up and Jess felt sure he would call her down or come up to her, but before he could, a body blocked her line of sight.

She knew before her eyes even reached his face that it was Randall. His plaid shirts were his trademark, and today he wore a blue and green plaid button down.

"Can I walk you to math?" he asked.

Discreetly, Jess leaned to the left as she grabbed her bag and glanced down to the front of the room, but Chad was gone.

Disappointment washed over her, but she knew she'd be seeing him later. "Sure, that would be fine," she said and followed Randall out the door.

It was mid-October. A chill had descended this week, making the air outside cooler than normal. Jess shivered as the cold seeped through her jacket. Pulling up the collar, she stepped a little faster. Randall matched her pace.

"So, I know you usually do a Bible study on Friday nights," he said, "but I was wondering if you'd like to go to a movie with me this weekend."

"I'd like to, Randall, but I'm kind of seeing someone."

Though his face fell slightly, he nodded. "Oh, yeah, of course you are. I should have known that."

Jess's heart went out to him. He was nice, and he deserved someone. But even if she had been single, she felt no emotions that way toward Randall.

~

"What was with the guy cornering you after class?" Chad asked Jess that evening as they sat together in the cafe of his dorm.

"Randall?" she asked after she finished chewing the French fry she had just stuck in her mouth. "He wanted to ask me out."

"What did you say?" Chad asked, trying to keep the jealousy he was feeling from showing in his voice.

"I told him I was seeing someone,"

she said, picking up another fry. A feeling of relief doused his jealousy, but it was short lived as Jess continued, "That brings up a good question though. Should I stay in your class now that we're dating? I mean what if someone finds out and claims special treatment or something?"

Chad hadn't thought about that aspect of it. There was probably some policy against dating students. "Yeah, you might have to change classes, though it will be so much harder teaching without seeing you there every day."

"You'll still see me every day," she said with a smile.

"I know, but it isn't quite the same."

"Ooh, hey, do you want to come to the Bible study Friday night? You can meet the rest of Emily's friends."

"I'd love that," Chad said. Three weeks ago, going to a Bible study would have made him cringe or run the other direction. However, after re-dedicating his life to God, he found he wanted to do anything and everything he could to learn more.

"Good." Jess popped another fry in her mouth and smiled.

CHAPTER 17

*A*s the days went on, Jess threw herself into studying the Bible and praying. Even though she was dating Chad, the need to discover herself echoed continually at the back of her mind. She'd gone from being abused to using and being used and was just now figuring out how to be useful to God. Of course, the child growing inside her complicated that, but still she felt… free.

She no longer slept until noon. Her mornings began at nine with a healthy breakfast and silent time with the Lord. After that, she would head to class - Psychology was a lot less interesting now that she'd switched out of Chad's class, but at least she still saw him most evenings.

After classes, her job at the Student Union filled the remaining afternoon hours. It had been a godsend, giving her money for food and her phone, which was getting a lot more use now that she had friends. Plus, the monotonous work gave her time to reflect and pray.

As she finished for the evening, she shrugged on her coat. Fall in Texas was unpredictable, and the last few days had felt more like the early tinges of winter than late November.

Her stomach growled as she stepped into the cool, crisp air. Instinctively, she placed her hand on her belly. There had been no discernible movement yet, only strange fluttering sensations that often caused her to pause.

"Are you all right?"

Jess would have known his voice anywhere. Her eyes lifted from her abdomen to Chad, clad in jeans and his trademark black leather jacket, and she smiled. He held a wrapped box in his hands.

"Is it the baby?" he asked, his eyes dropping to Jess's midsection, but not with his usual smolder. This time concern colored his gaze.

"Yeah, but you can't feel the movements from the outside yet. It's just a weird fluttery sensation in my stomach. It's hard to explain, but it's a little like butterflies flying around in there."

He looked at her, a strange expression on his face. "Do you" - he shoved his hands in his pockets and glanced down at the ground before meeting her eyes again

- "Do you ever think about keeping it? The baby, I mean."

"All the time, but we're so young, Chad. I don't know if it would be best for the baby."

"Oh. Yeah, you're probably right. Have you picked parents yet?"

Jess shook her head. She hadn't even gone back to the adoption center since the first visit. She knew she needed to, but something kept her from being able to finish the adoption process. "What's in the box?" she asked, switching the path of the conversation. She needed more time to think about the adoption before she could really discuss it. Even with him.

His eyes lit up. "Oh, it's for you," he said, holding it out to her. "It's a one-month present, and my way of apologizing that I have to work over most of break and can't take you home to meet my family."

Jess smiled as she took the box. She'd been disappointed when Chad told her he had to work over Thanksgiving break and would only be going home for Thanksgiving Day. Jess stated she wouldn't mind being alone the other days, but Chad insisted he wouldn't be able to work knowing she was all alone. Thankfully, Emily offered to take Jess to her home. That was a nice second choice though she hoped she would get to meet Chad's family soon.

She tore into the paper and opened the box to find a smart, black leather jacket similar to Chad's.

"It's for when we go riding," he said. "You seemed cold the last time. Plus, this will offer much more protection."

"Thank you," she said as her eyes filled with tears. Was this what it was like to have a real relationship? To have someone who truly cared about her?

"Hey, it's not supposed to make you cry," he said, pulling her close and wiping a tear from her cheek.

"Don't worry; they're happy tears," she said as she leaned up to kiss him. The feel of his lips on hers sent tingles down her spine.

"Oh, good. I was worried there for a second," he said as they parted. "Here, let's try it on." Chad helped her pull the coat out of the box, shrug out of her old one, and put on the new one.

The feel of the leather was cold on her arms at first, but it warmed quickly. However, when Jess tugged on the zipper, she realized quickly the coat wouldn't fit much longer. Not when her belly got much larger.

"Well, I guess we'll have to get another one in a few months," he said. "Now, let's get you inside. It's getting cold out here."

As his arm wrapped around her shoulders, Jess snuggled against his chest, enjoying the warmth and security he provided.

~

*C*had smiled as they walked back to Jess's dorm. He was pleased she liked the jacket and it looked good on her, but they would have to continue this discussion of the adoption. Ever since he had heard the first heartbeat with Jess, his desire to keep the baby had grown. She might not be ready, but he was beginning to think he was.

He would have to tread lightly with Jess though. She hadn't revealed everything to him, but he had a feeling her fear of raising the baby had a lot to do with her home life. Jess never talked about it, and the one time he had asked her, she had clammed up and changed the subject which only solidified his hunch.

Her dorm came into view too quickly. Chad had been hoping to take Jess home to meet his family, but Dr. Warren had gotten sick and tasked him with covering another class for the rest of the semester. He needed to spend the majority of the break working, and while he planned to return home for Thanksgiving dinner itself, he didn't want Jess having to be alone in her dorm room the rest of the break.

"Have a good trip," he said, giving her another kiss - a longer one this time as it had to last him four days. It did not disappoint, and as he watched her walk into her dorm, he wondered how he was going to make it the next few days without her.

CHAPTER 18

"You ready?" Emily asked as she zipped up her suitcase.

"Are you sure they'll be okay with me tagging along?" Jess asked as she rolled up the last shirt. Because she had nowhere to go and Chad had to work, Emily had invited Jess to her family's house for Thanksgiving.

"Of course they'll be okay. My house was the hangout during high school anyway."

"But, do you think they'll care, you

know, about the baby?" Jess was now in the second trimester and starting to show and though Emily and her friends accepted her, Jess still worried what others thought. With no ring on her finger, did they condemn her or pity her?

"I'm adopted, remember?" Emily asked with a smile. She crossed the short distance between them and flung her arm about Jess's shoulders. "Stop stressing about what others think about you. You made a mistake, you repented, and now you are making the best out of a difficult situation. A lot of women wouldn't make the choice you did. I'm proud of you and any true Christian would be too."

Her words soothed a few of Jess's insecurities and she pulled the drawstring of her duffel bag closed. As she passed the mirror on the way out of the room, Jess glanced at her reflection. The tough exterior might be fading away, but the insecure girl underneath still resided there. *God, grant me confidence,* she thought as she shut the door behind her.

$\sim$

*E*mily's house was a two-story brick home on the outskirts of Dallas. After the six-hour drive, it felt good to stretch. Jess's belly wasn't big yet, but it was larger than she was used to and so getting comfortable in the car had been harder than usual.

The girls grabbed their bags from the trunk and approached the front door. "You ready?" Emily asked as she opened the door. Jess offered a small smile in response.

Emily's house was warm and inviting and smelled of chocolate chip cookies. Emily led the way to the kitchen where a blonde woman who, surprisingly, resembled Emily greeted them. How could they look so similar while not being blood related? "Emily," she said with a wide smile.

"Hi, Mom," Emily said, returning the hug her mother had engulfed her in. "This is my roommate, Jess."

The woman turned her friendly green eyes on Jess. "Hello, Jess, and welcome to our home."

"Thank you for having me," Jess said.

"Oh, Emily's friends are always welcome here. Emily probably told you our house was the unofficial hangout when she was in high school."

Jess smiled at Emily. "Yeah, she did."

"Okay, let's go drop off these bags," Emily said leading the way to her old room. Trophies and medals lined shelves hanging on the walls.

"Wow, you really are an athlete," Jess said. She had never won a trophy or a medal unless you counted the ribbons in elementary school they gave out on field days.

"Yeah, I played a lot, but you want to know a secret?" she asked as she hefted her suitcase on the bed.

"Sure." Jess glanced around the small room looking for a place to drop her stuff. A brown, roll-top desk took up most of one wall and while there was a window seat under the two windows, it didn't look large or comfortable enough to sleep on.

"Oh, it's a trundle," Emily said, evidently noticing Jess's questioning gaze. She lifted the flowered bed skirt and pulled out a second twin mattress on a rolling platform. When it was free from the bed, she motioned Jess over. "Here, help me out. There's a bar we have to press to get it to raise."

Jess reached under where Emily was holding and felt a cold metallic bar. As the girls pressed it up, the mattress raised as if on a lift until it was even with Emily's bed.

"We'll get you some sheets and a blanket later, but for now you can put your stuff there," she said, pointing to the mattress.

As Jess placed her bag on the mattress, she returned to the previous conversation, "So, what's the secret you were going to share?"

Emily smiled a sentimental smile. "I kind of feel like I missed childhood. If I could go back, I might take some time off, not play so many games, and just be a kid, you know?"

Jess knew. Not that she would go back to High school, but she would love to go back to early childhood, when her mom was sober, and it was just her mother and her. Her mom had worked a lot then, but at least she was present every evening. She'd read Jess stories and tucked her in and on weekends she would make smiley face pancakes.

"Ready to meet the rest of the family?" Emily asked, breaking into Jess's reminiscing.

Jess nodded, but as she followed Emily back into the kitchen, she couldn't help wondering if she could be a mother like that - the good kind. Like before her mother had found solace for her loneliness in a bottle. Or would she end up as her mother eventually had, broken and overwhelmed? Her mother had been a teen mom and Jess knew there was sometimes a cycle to these things, but could she break it and keep her child?

～

The smell of turkey and sweet potatoes greeted Chad as he walked into the house.

"You're home," his sister, Kendra, yelled as she accosted him in the hallway.

"I told you I would be," he said with a laugh, returning her hug. When he'd recommitted his life to Christ, he had also recommitted to his family, calling them at least once a week to keep them informed.

He'd told them about Jess, but he hadn't mentioned the baby yet. It wasn't that he was hiding it, but he felt that Jess needed to be there when he had that conversation. Plus, he wanted to be firm in his decision of either keeping the baby or putting him or her up for adoption before telling them.

"Come on," she said, tugging on his arm. "Lunch is almost ready, and the football game is on."

Chad smiled as he followed her. It felt good to be home, and while he missed Kyle, he was glad to have his family back in his life.

"Hello, Son," his mother said as he entered the kitchen. She dropped the spoon she was stirring a pot with and walked over to envelop him in a hug. "When are we going to meet this mysterious girlfriend of yours?"

"Soon," Chad said. "I would have brought her with me, but I have to work when I get back and I didn't want her stuck alone in her dorm room."

"Well, that was very chivalrous of you," his sister spoke up, "but I'm starting to wonder if she's even real."

"All right, that's enough," his mother said as Chad lunged playfully at his sister. "It's dinnertime, so why don't the two of you go join your father at the table?"

The table was overflowing with platters of food, from turkey and stuffing to sweet potatoes and green bean casserole. Once again, his mother had cooked enough for an army - a trait she'd had for as long as Chad could remember.

A pang of sadness washed over him as he glanced at Kyle's empty chair. This would mark the third Thanksgiving without him and Chad wondered if it would ever get easier. But he didn't have time to focus on his sadness long as his father greeted him with a hug and his mother and sister took their places around the table.

"Frank, would you pray for us?" his mother asked.

"Actually, Mom, can I do it?" Chad spoke up.

She flashed him a smile and though she said nothing, Chad could tell she was glad to finally have her prodigal son back home again.

~

"So, Emily tells me you're planning on putting the baby up for adoption," Emily's mother said as Jess helped wash the dishes that evening. Jess had offered to help clean up as a thank you for allowing her to come and crash at their house.

"I honestly don't know anymore," Jess said with a sigh. "I know adoption is the smart move because I'm young and single and know nothing about raising a baby. However, as my belly grows and I feel the strange movements, I think about what he or she might look like. Then I wonder if I'll be strong enough to give the baby away. And the baby's father is back in the picture which makes it even harder."

With a nod, her mother turned wise eyes on her. "I'm sure you're not alone in that feeling. I can't imagine how hard it must be for you to feel the baby growing and know you won't get to see him or her grow up. Have you tried praying about it?"

"Every day," Jess said with a sad smile. "Maybe I'm doing something wrong though. I thought I would hear an answer or see something like I did when I tried to destroy Emily's Bible." Her mother raised an eyebrow. "It's a long story," Jess continued with a laugh, "but I haven't felt or heard or seen anything. Is that normal?"

"You know, a lot of people think they can ask God a question and hear an answer like we're talking right now, but He doesn't really work like that usually. Sometimes, the answer will come in feelings like you'll feel conflicted if it's not the right decision."

Jess shook her head. "I feel conflicted with both decisions, so I'm not sure that helps."

Emily's mother smiled as she continued, "Sometimes the answer will come through actions of others. Someone you know will do or say something that makes the answer clear." No, Jess wasn't having that either. "And sometimes, you'll actually hear God speak to you, but He speaks in a still, small voice, so you have to be very focused on listening for it. I know it seems confusing now, but I'm willing to bet that God will reveal Himself when He's ready."

Jess took that nugget of wisdom to bed with her that night and chewed on it over and over in her head as she lay in the foreign room. Was she trying to rush God's timing? The pastor had often spoken about God's upper plan being different from what we could see down here, and maybe even though time felt short for her, it surely wasn't for God.

CHAPTER 19

*J*ess's phone rang as they were driving back to Lubbock. She smiled as she recognized Chad's number. Though they had spoken a few times over the break, the conversations had been short, so he could work. She was looking forward to seeing him again tonight. "Hello, Chad."

"Hey Jess, will you be home by seven?"

Jess looked at her watch. It was barely one. They had headed back right after church ended. "Yeah, we should be home by six barring traffic."

"Great. Will you meet me at the Starbucks on University at seven?"

"Sure, but what's up?" She had expected to hang out in his dorm, not at a coffee shop. What did that mean?

"I don't want to tell you over the phone. Please? It's important."

"Okay. I'll see you at seven." As Jess hung up the phone, she couldn't help but wonder what the secrecy was about. Her old insecurities seeped in. Had Chad found someone else while she was gone? Had their whole relationship been a sham?

"What was that about?" Emily asked.

"I have no idea," Jess responded with a slow shake of her head. "I guess I'll see at seven."

*C*had sat a table in the coffee shop and tapped his finger against the table top. The last few hours had crawled by as he waited for seven to hit. His visit home had solidified his feelings, and he knew now he wanted to raise his child. He hoped Jess would feel the same, but he could no longer sign adoption papers.

A chill breeze swept through the room and Chad glanced up. Jess stood in the entrance scanning the room. His face lit up at the sight of her and he crossed quickly to embrace her.

Her arms wound around his neck as she returned his kiss, and a heat spread through his body. "I've missed you," he said as they parted.

"I missed you too," she said with a smile.

"Come, sit down," he said, taking her hand and leading her to the table he had been sitting at. "Would you like a coffee or something to eat?"

"No, I'm okay. What's going on, Chad?"

His eyes held her gaze a moment and then dropped to the tabletop where his finger tapped again. After a deep breath, he raised his eyes again. "I know I said I wasn't ready to raise a child, but after going home on Thursday and seeing my parents, I've found myself daydreaming about you and the baby and us as a family."

He paused, waiting for Jess to say something, but she only blinked at him.

"I guess what I'm saying is I don't want you to give the baby up for adoption. I want us to raise the baby together. I want what my parents have."

"Chad, I'm so young. I'm only nineteen," Jess began.

"I know we're young," he said

interrupting her, "but younger people than us have done it. I'm almost out of school, and I can support you while you finish." His eyes pleaded with hers.

"But why? Why do you want this baby so badly?"

His gaze was frank and unwavering as he stared into her eyes. "Because I love you, and I see my future with you. I honestly think we'll regret the decision if we give this kid away. Our family will never feel complete, you know?"

Jess looked as though she was going to object again, but Chad jumped in before she could.

"Let's at least try," he pleaded.

"Okay, let's try," she said with a laugh.

He reached across the table and grabbed her hands, sending a tingling sensation down his arm. "I know you think I'm crazy, and maybe I am, but I'm also serious about this."

"Okay, let's raise a baby."

"I'll show you, Jess. I'll show you I can be father material. I still have some prep work for tomorrow, so I have to run, but let's do dinner tomorrow."

~

*J*ess nodded at him, still unable to find the right words. He squeezed her hands and then stood and walked away, leaving her in a happy but dazed stupor as she watched him leave.

In her pocket, her phone rang. Still reeling from the last few minutes, Jess tapped the answer button without looking at the caller ID. "Hello?"

"Jess?"

Her mother's voice caused the hair on Jess's arms to stand up. What did she want? And did Jess even care what she had to say? The broken part of her wanted to ignore the call, to pretend it had never occurred and just hit the end call button now, but the other part of her —the part that God was healing— decided she should at least see what her mother wanted.

"Yes, it's me. What's... what's going on?" What was with today? First Chad and now her mother? Could it get any stranger?

"I wanted to see if I could come see you. I kicked Jim to the curb. You were right about him. I'm sorry I didn't listen to you."

Jess held the phone away from her ear and stared at it. As much as she wanted to believe her mother, so much hurt existed between them. If she gave her mother another chance, would she just end up hurt again? A tiny voice inside her head whispered "forgiveness," but there was so much pain in the past.

A sudden bolt of inspiration hit her, and she responded, "Yeah, I guess you can come, but only if you come to church with me." Jess knew this would dissuade her mother if she weren't serious.

Silence descended.

"I didn't know you were attending church." Her mother's voice was hesitant, soft.

"I am now. I am trying to repair the damage you did to my life, so take it or leave it. You want to see me, then you come to church. Otherwise, don't bother."

"Fine, I'll drive up Saturday morning. We can spend the day together and attend church the next morning."

Jess agreed and hung up the phone. Shock rolled off her in waves. What had she just agreed to? Her hands began to shake, and the urge for a cigarette gripped hard even though she hadn't smoked in a month. Trying to focus on anything else, Jess stared out the window.

"Jess?"

She turned around to see Chase staring down at her, wearing the traditional green apron of Starbucks' employees. How had she missed seeing him when she walked in? "Yes, hi, how are you?"

"I'm good, are you okay? Can I get you something?"

"Um,"—she was about to tell her usual—coffee, black with one sugar, but she caught herself, "Sure, I'd love a green tea." She could have ordered a decaf, but it wouldn't be the same, so she might as well have a tea instead.

"Not a coffee fan?" he asked smiling.

"Something like that."

He returned a moment later, and she

cupped her hands around the mug, enjoying the warmth that traveled up her arms. She sipped the steaming liquid as she tried to make sense of the last ten minutes.

When her drink was finished, she began the walk back to the dorm. The last half hour felt like a dream, but perhaps telling Emily would help it feel more real.

CHAPTER 20

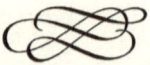

*J*ess stood in front of the closet, surveying the dark contents. Even though she was no longer wearing mostly black, she still preferred darker colors, but nothing was jumping out at her today. What did you wear when you hadn't seen your mother in months and the last time you did was shrouded with anger and disbelief?

Deciding on a simple long-sleeved blue shirt, Jess pulled it and some jeans on. She was only a few months along, but already her jeans were starting to fit snugly. She would have to buy some new ones soon.

A look in the mirror revealed the fear and insecurity in her blue eyes, but there was no turning back now. As much as she wasn't sure she wanted to see her mother, she didn't feel okay leaving her sitting in a restaurant waiting either.

"You look good," Emily said from her side of the room. "Are you sure you don't want me to go with you?"

Jess shot her a grateful look and shook her head. This, she had to do alone. Taking a deep breath and sending words heavenward for wisdom, Jess headed out of the room and to the coffee shop she had agreed to meet her mother at. It was the same coffee shop she had met Chad at just a week before.

As she pushed open the dorm door, a gust of cool wind blew against her, causing goosebumps to rise on her arms. She should have worn a heavier coat, but the walk wasn't far.

By the time Jess reached the coffee shop, her cheeks were numb and probably pink from the cold. She pulled open the door and scanned the shop. Her mother was not one of the patrons, and Jess sighed in relief.

Chase was working the counter again, and his smile calmed the jitters running through her. After ordering a tea, she took the cup to an empty table and sat down to wait. The liquid warmed her insides, dispelling the last lingering tendrils of cold.

Her mother walked in a few minutes later, and Jess almost didn't recognize her. Her dark hair was combed and had regained some of its sheen. Her blue eyes appeared unclouded and focused. Had she gotten off drugs? Her lips curled in a small smile as she stepped in Jess's direction.

Jess had forgotten how much she looked like her mother. The resemblance was unnoticeable when she was on drugs. But now her mother looked clean, and Jess could see what she might look like in another fifteen years.

"Hi Jess." Her mother stood awkwardly. Jess stared at her, unsure if she were expecting a hug or just awaiting an invitation to sit. She pointed to the chair, not ready to embrace her mother yet.

"You look good," her mother said, pulling out the chair and sitting down. "Different."

"Yeah, I am different," Jess said. "You look good too."

Her mother's eyes dropped to the grey tabletop. "Thanks," she said softly, "it's because of you. When you left, I... uh I didn't know what to do. I got worse for a while, I think, but then Stephanie told me Jim was touching her too. I remembered your words, and I stopped taking drugs and started paying attention. You were right about Jim, and I'm so sorry I didn't believe you. When I realized I couldn't ignore Stephanie too, I knew I had to take her, leave, and get completely clean. I just hit my ninety-day's clean milestone."

"That's great, Mom, I'm happy for you." The words sounded insincere because while happy for her mother, Jess was also guarded and still angry. Her mother had given up drugs a few times before, but it had never lasted.

"I know it will take time, but I want to see if I can be a part of your life again."

Jess was tempted to tell her no, that she had been hurt too often. However, she had learned that God was about forgiveness, and that if she were forgiven, she should forgive her mother as well. It wasn't easy as the words lodged in her throat, but eventually she managed. "I'd like that."

"I'd like to hear how your year is going…. If you don't mind telling me about it," she said.

Jess dropped her eyes to her cup and twirled it around. Did she tell her mother about the baby? It was a pretty important piece of her life, but did she want to share that information yet?

"My year has been interesting to say the least," Jess began slowly, deciding that if her mother were making an effort to be in her life that she could make an effort to trust her. "But I guess the most important thing to tell you is that I'm pregnant."

Her eyes widened, and her hand flew to her open mouth. "You are?"

"I'm having the baby," Jess said. "We didn't do it right the first time, but we are committed to following God's way now."

"We?" Her mother asked. "So, the father is in the picture?"

"He is," Jess said. "You can meet him at church tomorrow."

Jess waited for her mother to balk or come up with an excuse not to go, but she smiled and said, "I can't wait. You obviously found a part of religion I never knew and I'm looking forward to finding out what it is."

"It's not about religion, Mom. It's about Jesus." Jess smiled as she continued to share the story with her mother of how she came to know Christ.

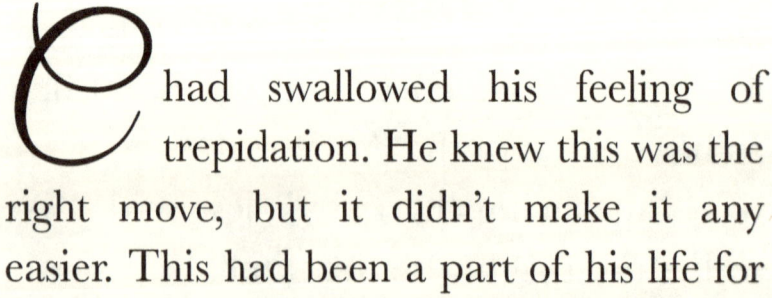

Chad swallowed his feeling of trepidation. He knew this was the right move, but it didn't make it any easier. This had been a part of his life for the last few years and he wasn't sure who he would be without it.

"Can I help you?" The salesman was an older man with a pot belly and a bald spot.

"Yeah, I need a car," Chad said. "A nice, safe, economical, family car."

"Yeah? We got lots of those. Follow me."

The man led Chad through the parking lot to the used car section. After test driving a few and haggling over the price, Chad followed the man into the sales office and spent the next half hour filling out forms.

CHAPTER 21

*W*hen Sunday rolled around, Jess couldn't tame the butterflies in her stomach. Would her mother really go to church with them?

"You ready?" Emily asked with an encouraging smile.

Jess swallowed and nodded.

At the base of the stairs, Chad waited, looking more handsome than Jess had ever seen him. His black leather jacket still graced his shoulders, but underneath he wore a blue button-down shirt that enhanced the color of his eyes, and a pair of black slacks that accentuated his other assets. This was not his first time attending church, but it was the first time he had dressed so nicely.

"Wow," Jess breathed. "You clean up nice."

"Thank you," he said. His normal bravado was missing from his voice, but the remaining tone was rich and silky. He closed the distance between them and met Jess at the stairs as her feet were still not cooperating. Taking her hand, he locked eyes with her. "I told you I would prove I was father material to you. This is just step one."

As he led the way out to the parking lot, Jess wondered what he had in mind for the other steps.

"Uh, my car is this way," Emily said, pointing to the right.

"I thought we'd take my mine," Chad

said with a smile as he led them to a silver Chevy Traverse.

"When did you get a car?" Jess asked. The only vehicle he had ever talked about was his Harley.

"Yesterday, when I sold my Harley."

Jess's jaw dropped. "You sold your motorcycle? But I loved riding it with you."

"Do you have a car?" Chad asked in a teasing tone.

"Well, no, I sold mine to help pay bills when I moved out of my mom's house," she said.

He squeezed her arm and smiled. "Then one of us needed a car to put a car seat in. We can always get another motorcycle later when we can afford it."

Jess blinked at him. The baby wasn't even due until late summer and he was already thinking about car seats?

"Besides, in a few months, you'll be

too big to ride behind me," he said with a glint in his eye.

Jess playfully slapped his arm, but he was right. In another few months, holding on to him would have become a problem.

"All right you love birds," Emily said. "Let's get going. We still need to get your mom, right, Jess?"

"Yes, we do," Jess agreed. "You don't mind, do you?"

～

*C*had didn't mind. In fact, he was super curious to meet anyone from Jess's family. She had only ever mentioned her mother, but even those mentions had been few and far between.

He pulled into the hotel parking lot Jess directed him to and parked the car. "Do you want me to go with you?"

She shook her head. "No, I'll run in

and grab her and be right back." Jess jumped out of the car before he could say anything else and hurried into the hotel.

"Have you met her yet?" Chad asked, turning to Emily.

"No, but I hope for Jess's sake she really has changed."

Chad wondered what that meant and made a mental note to ask Jess later. If they were going to do this right, he needed to know all of her, even the stuff she wanted to keep hidden.

A few minutes later, Jess and an older woman emerged. Other than the few grey streaks sprinkled throughout her hair and the few extra wrinkles on her face that hinted at her older age, the woman could have passed for Jess's older sister.

"Mom, this is my roommate Emily," Jess said as she opened the door and ushered her mother inside. "And this is my boyfriend, Chad."

"Nice to meet you both," the woman said. "You can call me Diane."

Chad hoped he would have the chance to ask Diane questions later. He had a lot for her, but for now, church awaited them, so after everyone was buckled in, Chad pointed the car that direction.

⁓

"What did you want to talk to me about?" Jess asked her mother as they walked around the campus. After church, the group had gone to lunch and then Chad had dropped them off at the dorm, so he could finish up work for the next day. Her mother had asked for a tour and Jess obliged, feeling the need to stretch her legs.

"I uh need to ask you for a favor," her mother said, dropping her eyes.

"I don't have any money, Mom," Jess said with disgust. She should have known it was too good to be true. Her mother was obviously about to ask for money for drugs.

"What?" her mother asked. "Oh no, Jess, I don't need money. I told you I'm clean. I need you to testify against Jim."

"No way!" Jess shook her head. "I've finally gotten past those memories and you've left him. Why on earth would I testify?"

"Because Stephanie needs you to. She will testify too, but the case would be much stronger with your added testimony. There's a chance he'll get away with it if it's just Stephanie's word. You know how persuasive he can be."

Jess shuddered at the memory. She knew firsthand how persuasive he could be. It was how he got so close to her before she realized what was happening.

"I don't know, Mom. I'll think about it, but I'm trying to put that behind me. There's a baby to think about now."

"I know, and I'm sorry to have to ask. I'll understand if you can't, but I truly think it might help with your healing as well," her mother said.

Jess bit her lip and shook her head. How was she going to heal if she kept having to revisit the nightmares of her past?

CHAPTER 22

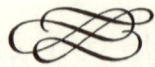

The crisp autumn air cooled as December hit. Jess had picked up a heavier jacket from a local thrift store as the weather forecast often threatened snow now, and her stomach had grown just enough that her leather jacket didn't zip. The new jacket kept her warm even though the wind had turned the air a little colder on the walk to and from class.

It was one of these especially chilly days when the semester ended. Jess zipped up her coat as far as it could go, and after throwing her backpack on, she jammed her hands into her pockets to warm them up as best as she could. Though the rooms were warmer than outside, her hands were like ice today.

As Jess pushed open the door and a wintry chill ambushed her, she wished she had bought a scarf at the thrift store too. Dropping her head, she braved the short walk back to the dorm, wishing there was a fireplace to warm up in front of. She'd have to throw on a heavier sweater and crawl under her covers to warm up. Jess was considering the quickest option when she heard her name being called.

Chad was hurrying after her, a smile lighting up his whole face. "I'm glad I caught you." His breath came out in labored gasps. How long had he been running after her? "My mother said there's a storm coming tomorrow, so are you okay if we head out tonight?"

Jess and Chad had planned to drive to Amarillo to spend Christmas with his family. Her nerves were in a bundle since it would be her first time meeting them.

"Sure, I'm mostly packed. Just have to give Emily her gift."

"Great, I'll swing by to get you in an hour after I finish packing." He leaned in and kissed the corner of her mouth before hurrying off toward his dorm.

Though it had been short, just the touch of his lips on hers had sent a warm sensation flowing through her body. Jess didn't think she'd ever tire of kissing him. She hurried the last of the way to the dorm, relishing the disappearing warmth from his lips and looking forward to the heat that the building would offer from the pervading cold outside.

"Hey," Emily said looking up from the suitcase she was packing as Jess entered.

"I will miss you." She was going home to Mesquite for the break.

"Me too, but it's only a few weeks," Jess said, putting down her backpack and pulling out her own bag to finish filling it. "Be sure to say hi to everyone in your family for me though. Oh, hey, before you go, I got you this." Behind her pillow, Jess had hidden a colorfully wrapped gift. She grabbed it and turned around, holding it out to Emily.

"I've got one for you too," Emily said, holding out her own box. Laughing, the girls exchanged boxes and ripped into the paper.

"Emily, it's beautiful," Jess sighed as she pulled out a delicate silver cross necklace. A small silver ribbon marked by tiny footprints wrapped around it. Ever since she had heard the Footprints in the Sand poem, she had loved the idea of it, and a cross that represented that was a perfect gift. Jess fastened it around her neck and touched the spot where it lay.

"I'm so glad you like it. I know mine always gives me peace, and I wanted the same for you." She finished unwrapping her gift and smiled. "Jess, thank you, my old one was getting so full."

Jess had found the perfect leather journal for Emily to write her prayer requests in. She held it to her nose sniffing the leather and smiled over the top.

"Oh, good. I didn't smell it, but I thought it was perfect," Jess said with a laugh. Emily crossed the room to throw her arms around Jess in a giant hug which Jess reciprocated until a knock at the door grabbed the girls' attention. "I'll get it," Jess said, crossing to the door.

Chad stood on the other side, his blue shirt making his eyes appear like the ocean after a storm. "Hey beautiful, are you ready?" He pulled her in, placing his lips on hers, longer this time. Sparks ignited in her body. "Hi Emily," he said when he finally separated from Jess.

"Hi Chad," she waved from the bed, smiling at the show and the blush that spread across Jess's face.

"Come on in, I'm almost ready," Jess said, recovering. She grabbed his hand and pulled him inside.

"Okay, I have to go," Emily said, finishing packing her bag. "Have a great break you two." She hugged them both before flying out the door.

Jess smiled at Chad as she shoved the last few things in her bag. This would be their first test at being completely alone since they had decided to no longer have sex. Chad had told her his family was religious, so she wasn't worried about anything happening at their house. However, it was a nearly two-hour drive there down stretches of road that were not always heavily populated. She and Chad were both growing in their relationship with God daily, but they were still both human and physically attracted to each other.

"All done," Jess said and zipped the bag closed. One final glance assured her nothing was plugged in or forgotten. Picking up her bag, Jess followed Chad out the door.

As soon as the door shut, Jess's nerves kicked in. Chad had told his family about her when he'd first told them of his decision to follow Christ again, but he hadn't told them about the baby, and they planned to today.

Jess's stomach wasn't that large, but they wouldn't be able to ignore it much longer. Chad had assured her his family would be sympathetic and understanding, but past experiences still filled her mind. Sensing her discomfort, Chad squeezed her hand and flashed an encouraging smile.

The ride to his family's house was quiet and comfortable with no stops along the less populated roads, but the nerves still tangled in Jess's stomach. Her throat grew drier the closer they got, and her head pounded as they pulled into his family's driveway. The SUV crunched over a light dusting of snow. Though it had missed Lubbock, Amarillo had gotten the tail end of the first storm that had passed through a few days ago.

Jess accepted Chad's help in climbing out of the truck and self-consciously ran her hands across her stomach as he crossed to the back of the truck to get the luggage. The blue coat she had picked up hid most of the protruding bump, but it would be seen as soon as the coat was removed.

"You look beautiful," Chad said,

rounding the truck with the suitcases and noticing her nervous gesture. Jess shot him a grateful smile as they ascended the steps. Though still the handsome and intriguing guy she had first met, Chad had accepted the role of encourager easily, which had only deepened her love for him.

"Chad," his sister shouted as the two entered. His sister was a freshman with long brown hair, big brown eyes, and wire-framed glasses. She threw her arms around Chad's neck, squeezing until he cried Uncle. "I knew I could get you one day," she said triumphantly before turning inquisitive eyes on Jess.

"Hey, Kendra, this is my girlfriend Jess."

Kendra stuck out her hand and smiled at Jess. "It's nice to meet you. After he came home for Thanksgiving alone, I wondered if you were even real."

Jess laughed and returned the handshake. "Well, here I am."

"Come on, Mom's making cookies," Kendra said before spinning around and dashing ahead of them down the hallway.

Chad and Jess continued into the kitchen where his mother was indeed rolling dough into little round balls. She had the same dark hair as Chad and his sister, and a warm smile.

"You must be Jess. I'm Tanya."

Jess nodded, expecting a handshake, but instead Chad's mother pulled her in for a hug. Jess's eyes widened as she realized his mother would feel the baby bump. The surprise registered on his mother's face as she pulled back, and Jess shot Chad a glance. They would have to spill the news even earlier than planned.

Chad took the hint and jumped in, grabbing his mother's attention. "Hey, Mom, is Dad around?"

His mother nodded, calling for her husband, Frank, to join them. She put the tray into the oven, set a timer, and wiped her hands on a nearby towel. His father, an older version of Chad, only with a full beard and salt and pepper hair, stepped into the kitchen and hugged Chad before turning to shake Jess's hand.

"Can we go in your office for a second?" Chad asked.

His mother and father exchanged a glance but nodded and led the way. Jess's heart thudded in her chest as they followed.

Frank's office was small, but inviting, decorated in earth tones. Family pictures lined the walls, giving it a homey feel as well.

The door shut, and Chad grabbed Jess's hand and gave it a squeeze. They had decided on the way here that she would start the conversation, but her throat was now dry and scratchy. A long swallow returned a semblance of peace, and she opened her mouth.

"Um, so I wanted to thank you both for inviting me to come and spend the holidays with you. My relationship with my mom is still a little rocky, but I wanted to be honest with you. I"—she glanced over at Chad—"We made mistakes before finding God this year, and, um, I'm pregnant."

Frank's eyes enlarged to the size of saucers. Tanya had probably already suspected this information, but her mouth pulled into a tight line.

"Jess was going to put the baby up for adoption," Chad said, stepping in, "but I convinced her to keep it. We're going to raise the child together."

"You're going to what?" His father's words exploded from his mouth causing his head to shake with the ferocity.

Tanya laid her hand on Frank's arm. "Is this what brought you back to God, Chad?" Her stoic face held no emotion, but her soft voice was full of love.

Chad nodded. "It started with Kyle's journal as I told you, but I really committed when Jess told me she was pregnant. I know we're young, but I couldn't get her out of my head. So, we started dating, but I kept thinking about the baby. When I came home for Thanksgiving and remembered how great it was to be a family, well, then this feeling covered me. I knew we had to keep the baby and be a family."

He squeezed Jess's hand again, and though the words were meant for his parents, he said them with his gaze locked on Jess. "I promised Jess I would clean up my act, and I have. We know we messed up, but we're trying to make it right."

Frank's face was still a few shades

darker than his normal color, but his mouth had closed and his anger was starting to fade.

"That is admirable," Tanya said. "It's not the way I hoped to become a grandmother, but if this event has brought you home, then I can't say I wish it hadn't happened." Frank nodded beside her though he appeared to be deciding if he should say more. "There will be no sharing of rooms while you are here under our roof though."

"No, ma'am. We haven't anyway since we got back together." A blush colored Jess's cheek as she offered up the intimate information.

"Good," his mother said. "Well, let's not let this news ruin our evening. We will pray for this baby and the path you now face, which will be harder, but not impossible. We're glad you have changed your paths though, and we hope the two of you will remember this as your relationship deepens."

"We will, Mom," Chad said, squeezing Jess's hand again and shooting her a soft smile. Relief flooded over her. She couldn't believe how amazing his family was being.

Chad's mom nodded. "Now, I need to finish baking cookies. How about you come and help me?" She grabbed Jess and pulled her back to the kitchen to finish helping with the cookies. Jess donned an apron, happily chipping in.

~

*A*fter dinner, Jess helped Tanya clear the dishes, and then Chad whisked her away for a walk.

"Don't go too far," his mother called after them. "The snow is supposed to hit any time now."

Jess and Chad shared a secret smile as they bundled up. The December air was crisp, and their breath rose in smoky wisps from their lips. A light dusting of white made the yard seem almost magical. Chad thought back to the many winters he and Kyle had built snowmen or had snowball fights.

"Your parents took the news better than I thought they would," Jess said as they walked up his driveway.

Chad chuckled and clasped her hand. "They're still angry or maybe disappointed is a better word, but too polite to show it while you're here."

"Is it hard?" she asked. "Being home where memories of your brother are stronger?"

"It's always hard," Chad said. "Some memories never go away." He saw a flicker of something cross her face and was just about to ask her what was wrong when a drop of coldness touched his cheek. He glanced up to see snow falling slowly from the sky.

"Come on, we better get back in before your mother freaks on us," Jess said, tugging on his hand.

Chad raised his face and stuck out his tongue, attempting to catch a snowflake. "Juth a thecond," he said. Laughing, Jess grabbed his arm and pulled him back to the house. They were still laughing as they tumbled through the front door.

"There you are. I was just about to send your sister after you. There's hot chocolate in the kitchen. Why don't you go warm up?"

After hanging up their coats, they wandered into the kitchen and poured two mugs of hot chocolate. The rest of the family was gathered in the living room, and Chad and Jess joined them, mugs in hand.

ess took a seat next to Kendra on the tan leather couch. Chad sat beside her. With a small smile, Kendra passed Jess a Bible, which she opened and followed along as Chad's father led a Bible Study. It felt a lot like the small group back home with Jared, Emily, Chase, and Sarah. More than that, though, it felt like home.

The Bible study had just concluded when Jess felt her phone buzzing in her pocket. She knew, without even pulling it out, who it was. Her mother had been calling all week and Jess had been avoiding her calls because she still didn't know what she wanted to do. However, since she didn't want her mother bugging her all break, she decided to take the call and tell her mother she needed more time.

"I should take this," Jess whispered to Chad. "I'll be right back."

His brow furrowed together in confusion, but he nodded and Jess slipped out of the room, punching the call button as she went.

"Hi, Mom," she said quietly as she walked down the hall to the room she'd be sleeping in.

"Jess? Oh, I'm so glad I finally got ahold of you. Why are you whispering?"

"Because I'm at Chad's house and I don't really want anyone to hear this conversation," Jess hissed.

"You haven't told him yet?" her mother asked.

"No, I haven't told him yet. If I tell him, I'll lose him. No man wants a woman with a past like mine. So, please stop calling me before you ruin everything."

"Jess, I need to know your answer.

They moved Jim's hearings up. They are happening next month."

"I'll think about it, Mom. I promise, but I have to go now." With that, Jess ended the call before her mother could say anything else.

"What's going on, Jess?" Chad said from the doorway.

She hadn't heard the door open and she cursed herself for not paying closer attention. "Nothing," she lied, letting the old habit sneak back in. She had once been a master at lying. "Just a professor who needed to speak with me about one of my finals."

Jess had no idea how much Chad had heard, but as his face dropped, she knew he had heard enough to not believe her story.

"That wasn't a professor, Jess," he said, and she cringed at the emotionless tone of his voice. "What's really going on? Is there someone else?"

"Is that what you think?" Jess asked. Anger boiled inside her. He was just like all the other men she'd known after all.

"I don't know what to think," he said. "You won't talk to me. You've been withdrawn ever since your mother came to visit. I thought maybe you were just worried about your finals, but they're over now, so what is it? What's going on with you?"

She knew she hadn't been acting completely normal, but she couldn't believe he would immediately think there was someone else. "You know what? If you think I could just jump to another guy, then maybe I should. It's all you'll ever see me as, right? The unfaithful tramp."

"Jess, stop," he said, shaking her shoulders. "I'm sorry. I shouldn't have said that, but I'm worried about you and I'm worried about this secret you're keeping from me."

The anger fizzled, and tears flooded Jess's eyes. "I can't tell you. It will change everything." She crumpled to the floor and dropped her face in her hands.

"Jess," he said, sitting beside her. "I don't care what's in your past. Whatever it is, we can make it through, but we won't make it if you keep secrets from me. That's no way to start a marriage."

"Marriage?" she asked, splaying her fingers enough to look at him.

"Yeah, marriage," Chad said with a lopsided grin. "This isn't quite how I planned it, but I was going to ask you to marry me, Jess Peterson." He reached into his pocket and pulled out a small black, velvet box.

Her breath caught in her throat, sending out a hitching sob as he opened the box. Inside was a small gold band with a single tiny diamond in the middle.

"I know it's not much," he said. "You deserve way more and one day I promise I'll get you a better ring, but I want us to be married before the baby comes."

"It's beautiful, Chad," Jess said as she dropped her hands, "but I can't say yes until I tell you everything. I should have told you before, but I'm so ashamed." With a final shaky inhale, Jess gathered her breath and began the story of her sordid past.

❧

*A*s Chad listened to her speak, an intense sadness filled his soul. No one should ever have to go through the unspeakable acts Jess had endured. That sadness was quickly replaced with anger when she reached the part about testifying.

"That monster's still alive?" Chad hissed.

"He is," Jess said, "and I have the chance to speak at his hearing. My testimony could put him away, but I'm not sure I can do it."

Chad took her chin in his hands. "Jess, you are the strongest woman I know. You can do this, and I will be right there by your side."

"You mean you still want me?" Jess asked, her voice incredulous.

"Of course, I still want you," Chad said. "None of what happened was your fault. You were a victim. It doesn't change my opinion of you one bit, except maybe to make me love you even more. So, will you accept my proposal now and agree to be my wife?"

"Your proposal could use some work," Jess said with a laugh.

"I'll keep that in mind," he said, pulling out the ring. "Though in my defense, this was not the proposal I had planned."

"I'm sorry I ruined it," Jess said.

"You didn't ruin anything," Chad said. "I don't care about the proposal as long as the answer is yes. So, is it?"

"Yes," Jess said as he slid the ring on her finger. "It's a yes."

CHAPTER 23

"Okay, so we have the church booked and the pastor taken care of," Tanya said as she tapped the pen against the paper. "What am I missing?"

"Invitations," Jess said. "I know we're calling people since it's such short notice, but I'd still like to send out traditional invitations to your friends and family since we have a few weeks, and I'd like to have one as a keepsake."

"What about your friends and family?" Tanya asked.

"We can send one to my mom," Jess answered, "but all my friends are the people I've met this year, and I don't know their dorm addresses, except Emily's and that's only because it's my address too. Besides, most are probably home on break, and I don't even know where all of them call home."

"Okay then," Tanya said, scratching the pen across the paper. "We'll have fifty made to send out to our side of the family. That leaves…."

"Cake," Kendra answered entering the room. She had a bag of carrots in her hand. Jess bit back a smile because over the last few days, she had learned Kendra was obsessed with food. Jess rarely saw her without something in her hand though it was usually healthy. And on the few occasions she wasn't eating, she was chomping on gum.

"Right, cake," Tanya said, adding it to

the list. "We can visit some shops today and taste some. I'm not sure if they'll be backed up, so we better do it as soon as possible. Also flowers. I'm not sure what you had in mind, but we should look into those quickly too."

Jess had no idea what she had in mind. She had honestly never thought about marriage after her mother's failed attempts, so there had been no girly daydreams growing up. And she had only been engaged for five days, so she'd had little time to think of what she wanted, but she understood the need to rush the planning.

She and Chad had agreed they wanted to have the wedding before the baby's birth and that pretty much left weekends, Spring Break, or the rest of winter break. Doing it on a weekend had just seemed too hectic, and Jess had opted for winter break over Spring Break so that she wouldn't be huge walking down the aisle. Though most of her friends already knew about the baby, she still fought the emotions of feeling like people were judging her and getting married while she was still only slightly showing would help with that. Plus, since college breaks were longer, it gave them nearly a month to plan the wedding before classes started again.

"Can we look at a dress too?" Jess asked quietly. "I don't have much money, but hopefully there's a rental store or something around here that I can afford."

Tanya put down the pen and crossed to Jess. "Actually, my dear, Frank and I would like to buy your dress as a wedding gift to you."

"Oh, I couldn't let you do that," Jess said.

"No, we want to. It was always our plan to pay for the honeymoon, but since it seems you two won't be having one right away, we would like to do this instead."

Jess shook her head. "I don't know what to say."

"Say thank you," Kendra said and then chomped down on her carrot stick.

"Thank you," Jess said, blinking back the tears that had suddenly filled her eyes.

~

C had walked in as Jess ran a hand across her eyes. "Hey, what's this? I thought this was going to be a happy day."

"It is," Jess said. "Your mom offered to buy my dress."

A feeling of deep gratitude filled Chad, and he mouthed a silent thank you at his mother. He knew Jess had little money and her mother was still getting on her feet. "Sweet. When do we go?"

"You can't go with her to pick the dress," Kendra said. "You can't see the bride before the wedding, remember?"

"So, I'm stuck here all day while you all have the fun?" he asked.

"No, you can come with us to pick the cake, flowers, and invitations," his mother said. "Then you can do something else while we pick the dress."

"Sounds good," Chad said. Ever since their big conversation and the proposal five days ago, Chad hadn't wanted to let Jess out of his sight. Though he knew it was unfounded, a tiny piece of him worried she would change her mind and run away. He had been glad when she opted for the quick wedding.

"Great. Are we ready now?" Kendra asked. "I could use some cake."

Chad and Jess shared a glance and

snickered.

"What?" Kendra asked. "What's so funny?"

"Nothing," Chad said. Telling her would ruin the fun of teasing her.

"Let's go," his mother said, glancing at her watch. "It's after ten already and we have a lot to do."

~

*I*t was after four by the time the group made it to the dress shop. Chad had excused himself to get a cup of coffee from the nearby cafe while the girls picked out a dress.

An older woman with a kind face approached them as they entered. "Hello, my name is Angela. What can I do for you today?" she asked.

"We are in need of a dress," Tanya said.

"Of course," the woman said, looking at Kendra. "Congratulations. What are you, about a six?"

"Oh, it's not for me," Kendra said with a laugh. "It's for my soon-to-be-sister-in-law, Jess, here."

The woman turned her attention to Jess.

While her eyes held no condemnation, Jess felt as if the woman was examining her.

"You're with child, are you not?"

"I am," Jess said softly, wanting to sink into the floor. Was this woman about to chide her for sex outside of marriage?

Angela smiled and reached for Jess's hand. "Congratulations, my dear. Now, you seem young. Am I right that money might be limited?"

"I'll be covering the cost of the dress," Tanya said.

"Wonderful. I believe I have just the

thing. Come with me."

Jess followed her to the right side of the store where rows of wedding dresses hung from metal bars.

"Let's see," Angela said, flipping through dresses. "I bet you're a six, right?"

"Well, maybe before the pregnancy," Jess said.

"We can adjust for that," Angela said. "Ah, here it is. I designed this custom wedding dress for a client, but she cancelled the wedding. I couldn't give her a refund as it was a custom order, but I can give you a discount on it." She pulled out a long white satin gown and handed it to Jess. "There's a dressing room right there," Angela said, pointing to a pink door. "Why don't you go try it on and see how it looks?"

Jess took the dress into the room, slipped off her clothes, and pulled the dress over her head. It was a simple dress that hung in a clean silhouette from her shoulders to her toes. The sleeves were a sheer fabric and a small line of pearls lined the neck of the dress. At her feet, the dress pooled in a white billow of fabric.

A look in the mirror elicited a small gasp from Jess. Though her baby bump was visible in the dress, the overall effect was stunning and drew the eye away from her midsection. Jess had never felt more beautiful. With tentative fingers, she opened the door and stepped out for the others to see.

"Oh, Jess," Tanya said with a sigh. "You are indeed a vision."

"It's perfect," Kendra agreed.

"I knew it," Angela said. Her hands were clasped together under her chin and a wide smile lit up her face.

"We'll take it," Tanya said.

CHAPTER 24

"Are you nervous?" Chad asked as they finished their Bible study. They had been doing one nightly since they arrived at his parent's house nearly a month before but opted for an extra one this morning before the wedding. Chad was glad because Jess seemed preoccupied. "Everything for the wedding is ready and in just a few short hours we will be husband and wife."

"It's not that," she said with a shake

of her head. Her sapphire eyes met his. "I'm excited to be marrying you, but I'm worried about the hearing. I know I said I could do it, but now I'm not so sure."

Chad sighed. Of course, the hearing against her stepfather was scheduled for just a few weeks after the wedding. She'd agreed to testify, but Chad knew it was only for Stephanie's sake. Jess held no desire to relive the abuse that had been inflicted on her.

"You know what we haven't done?" he asked. "We haven't prayed for him."

"Pray for him," Jess said with surprise. "What good will that do?"

Chad smiled and took her hand. "God has changed far harder hearts than your stepfather's, but it might also give you peace. Remember, God said to pray for our enemies? Perhaps praying for him will take away some of your nervousness."

"I'll try anything," Jess said. "I don't want this cloud to ruin our wedding."

Chad led the two of them in prayer for Jim and for Stephanie and Jess when they would have to testify. As he said 'Amen,' the feeling that he should continue praying for Jim settled on his shoulders and Chad determined it would be his priority until the trial.

~

"*J*ess, you look so beautiful," Emily said as Jess surveyed herself in the mirror.

Jess could hardly believe the transformation herself. Kendra and Emily had curled her hair and pinned it up in such a way that the shaved part was barely visible. Dark ringlets hung down and framed her face, and the touch of make-up Emily had applied completed the picture.

"You do too," Jess said, turning to her friend. "I'm so glad you were able to come for this."

"I wouldn't have missed this for the world."

A knock sounded and then the door cracked open. Kendra's face appeared in the space. "You ready? It's time."

"As I'll ever be," Jess said. She thought she would be nervous, marrying Chad, but she had woken this morning with a sense of peace. And everything had come together. The cake had arrived, the church was decorated, and everyone that was supposed to show up - had.

Jess grabbed her bouquet of red roses and sniffed them. She knew it was cliché, but red roses were the first flowers Chad had given her, and they seemed like a perfect fit for her wedding.

Emily grabbed the two similar bouquets of white flowers and handed one to Kendra. The contrast was beautiful. The two girls in their red dresses with white roses and Jess in her white dress with red roses. It had been Tanya's suggestion and Jess was more than pleased with the outcome.

Kendra led the way to the sanctuary doors where Chad's groomsmen waited. Jess knew it was unorthodox that she had no one to walk her down the aisle, but she'd never had a father figure growing up. However, God was her Father and she wanted the place beside her to belong to Him, even if He couldn't be physically seen.

As the music started, Kendra and Emily gave her a quick hug before taking the arm of their groomsman. Jess closed her eyes and sent up a prayer. "Lord, thank you for the many blessings you have given me. Thank you for taking our mistake and turning it into a gift. Lord, bless our marriage and help us be the husband and wife you want us to be."

A feeling of warmth surrounded her like the warmth from a soft fire. Jess flashed one last smile heavenward and then, when the music changed, she opened the door to the sanctuary. The crowd rose to their feet and Jess blinked at the number of people. She had only invited a handful. Were all the rest of these Chad's family and friends?

Her feet froze to the floor for a moment in fear, but then her eyes found Chad's, and a small voice whispered in her head, "Fear not, daughter, for I am with you."

That was all Jess needed. She began the walk down the aisle toward the man she loved.

"Dearly Beloved," the pastor began as

she reached the front, "we are gathered here today to join this man and this woman in holy matrimony."

The pastor continued, but Jess didn't hear the words as her focus was on Chad. She couldn't believe how much both of them had changed.

"I do," Chad said and placed the ring on her finger.

Jess blinked, startled. Were they already at 'I do?' She had missed more than she thought.

"Do you Jess Peterson take Chad Michaels as your lawfully wedded husband, to have and to hold, in sickness and in health, in good times and bad, for as long as you both shall live?"

"I do," Jess said, sliding Chad's ring on his finger.

"Then by the power vested to me by the great state of Texas, I now declare you husband and wife. You may kiss the bride."

As Chad's lips touched her own, the baby kicked in her stomach and Jess smiled. Everything was going to be okay.

CHAPTER 25

*C*had and Jess were unpacking the last box when Jess's phone rang. He looked up as she answered.

"Hello?" she said and then paused as the person on the other end spoke. "What's that, Mom?" Another pause and then her mouth dropped open. "What?… Are you sure?… Okay, thanks Mom."

Jess hung up the phone and looked at Chad with wide eyes.

"What is it?" he asked with concern.

"Is it the baby?" He rushed to her side, but Jess waved her hand in dismissal.

"It's Jim," she said slowly. "He confessed, so there's no hearing."

Elation flooded Chad, and he picked her up and swung her around. "That's wonderful news. I've been praying that God would resolve this and He did."

"Yes, I guess He did," Jess said with a smile. "I love you, Chad."

"I love you too, Mrs. Michaels," he said, setting her down before lowering his face to plant his lips on hers.

~

*J*anuary passed and with it, the threat of snow. Though the air was still chilly, the biting wind had calmed to a nibbling breeze. February arrived, and for the first time in a long time, Jess was looking forward to

Valentine's Day. Plus, this month, her ultrasound was scheduled. Though Jess was nearly certain she was carrying a daughter, she wanted the surety of the ultrasound.

On the morning of the appointment, butterflies zoomed in her stomach. She placed her hands on her stomach, hoping to feel the baby move again. The feeling was an unexplainable sensation, but one she wouldn't trade for the world, and today she'd get a grainy picture of the baby. Pulling out her newly acquired stretchy pants from the dresser she now shared with Chad, she pulled them on over her enlarging belly and headed out to meet him.

"You ready?" he asked as he set down his coffee mug and stood.

"Yeah, I think so. I'm nervous though," she said.

"Me too." He grabbed their coats,

"But it'll be fine, and we'll finally be able to start thinking about names."

Though Chad had been tossing names out - Jackson if it was a boy, Kayleigh if it was a girl - Jess had been unable to decide on a name until she knew for sure what they were having, but today she would finally know. She pulled on her coat and followed Chad out the door.

The parking lot was mostly empty as they pulled in. Jess hoped this meant they would get in and out quickly. After checking in at the small desk, they found two empty seats in the waiting room. Another pregnant woman and an older man sat in two other chairs.

A few minutes later, a blonde technician called Jess's name and led the way back, down a short hallway carpeted in gray to a small room. There was an exam table, a computer, and two chairs in the small room.

The technician took a seat at the computer and patted the bed. "Hop up and let's take a look."

Jess climbed on the exam table and laid back. Chad positioned himself on the other side of the bed from the technician who folded Jess's shirt up and poured a glob of blue liquid on her stomach.

"Sorry, it's a little cold," she said as Jess shivered. She picked up the wand attached to the computer.

As she touched the wand to Jess's stomach, the black screen lit up. The heartbeat was audible almost immediately, and Chad's mouth dropped as he watched the screen.

"Okay, I'm going to take some measurements first, and then I can look for gender if you want." She moved the wand back and forth, stopping to click some things on her computer. Jess strained her eyes to see what the shapes were, but the screen was so grainy that she wasn't sure if she was seeing an arm or a leg. The wand continued to move back and forth. "Okay, I'm all set, do you want me to see if I can tell the gender?"

"I want to know," Jess said and then looked at Chad, "Do you still want to see or wait?"

"See," he said. His answer was decisive and made her smile. They hadn't discussed whether they hoped for a boy or girl, but it was obvious he had been thinking about it.

A smile broke out on the technician's face. "Okay, let's see what we have." The wand moved again. "So, here's the head and the spine."

Jess looked closely at what the technician was pointing out, but she couldn't tell one white part from another.

She had never thought much about an ultrasound technician's job, but now it was obvious why they received so much training.

"Here are the legs, so let's see, well it looks like a little girl. Now, girls aren't as accurate as boys because the baby could just be hiding that part, but I'm pretty confident that you are having a girl."

Tears welled up in Jess's eyes. Somewhere deep inside, she had known she was having a daughter, but hearing the words triggered an emotion she hadn't even known was residing there.

The technician printed off a few ultrasound pictures and handed them to Jess. "Okay, I'm going to show some of the scans to the doctor just to make sure everything looks good and then you'll be free to go. Here's a towel you can use to clean your stomach."

She handed Jess a towel and left the

room, leaving Jess and Chad staring at each other, in awe of God's creation and the perfectness they could see in the tiny grainy images.

The technician returned a few minutes later with a smile on her face and a disc in her hand. "Okay, you're good to go and here's a video for you." She held out the disc.

"A video of what?" Jess asked.

"The ultrasound. Everything we did today. It's on video now."

Jess grabbed the CD, an unexplainable feeling surging through her body. "I didn't know they did this. Thank you."

CHAPTER 26

The rest of February, March, and April flew by. Jess and Chad had moved into a two-bedroom apartment in his building, and Chad spent the mornings teaching and the afternoons setting up the nursery or studying. Jess still worked at the student union, so he tried to have dinner ready for her when she returned home each night as well.

As May began, the uncomfortable stage of pregnancy hit for her. Jess's belly had now grown out far enough she could no longer see her feet, and she definitely couldn't lean over to tie shoes. She had asked Chad to tie her shoes for a few days, but finally had resorted to a pair of slip-ons.

A nasty case of heartburn had also started in the last month, and after burning through an entire bottle of Rolaids in one week, she had asked the doctor about it. The doctor had prescribed Ranitidine, which at least tamed the fiery beast enough that she could sleep. Unfortunately, she could no longer sleep in her favorite position, so she would often toss and turn keeping Chad awake.

It was after one such sleepless night that he had done some online research and found the perfect gift for Jess and himself.

"Come on," Chad said, grabbing her arm and pulling her to the Traverse. He had surprised her after her last class with a bouquet of flowers and a chocolate milkshake, her current weakness.

"I have work, Chad," she said, handing the flowers back to him. He noticed she kept the milkshake tight to her chest.

"Not today you don't. I talked to Darla and got you the afternoon off. Now, come on."

"Where are we going?" she asked before taking a large sip of the milkshake.

"It's a surprise." He grinned like a kid at Christmas waiting to open his first gift.

Smiling and shaking her head, Jess allowed herself to be pulled to the SUV and for him to open the door and help her climb in.

Ten minutes later, Chad pulled into the parking lot of a mattress store. Sleep City blazoned across the roof and two sheep decorated the front windows.

"Uh, Chad, I don't understand," she said, turning a raised eyebrow on him.

"Just wait," he said with a smile that sent his eyes sparkling in delight.

He jumped out of the SUV, nearly skipping to Jess's side to help her out. She followed him into the store, but confusion was still clearly written all over her face. Chad scanned the store for a salesman, and after gaining one's attention, he whispered a request to the man.

The man, a middle-aged, bearded man with glasses, nodded; his lips pursed, and then his eyes lit up. A smile etched across his face, and he motioned for Chad to follow him.

They followed him around several mattresses, bedroom furniture, and finally to the back of the store where pillows and linens lay. The salesman picked up a giant pillow, almost as tall as he was, and held it out to Jess.

"You want to buy me a pillow?" she asked in a hesitant voice. It was clear she had missed the gesture.

"Not just any pillow," Chad said. "This is a contouring body pillow. It's supposed to help pregnant women sleep better. My mom swore by one when she was pregnant with my little sister."

Jess smiled as the thoughtfulness of his gift sank in. "Thank you," she said with sincerity. "I can't wait to try it out."

~

"How are you feeling?" Emily asked from the living room as Jess dressed for the day. They had finished finals yesterday and had agreed to have a final hurrah to celebrate today.

"Like a giant melon," Jess said, entering from the bedroom. "I miss my feet. Do I have on matching shoes?" It was a running joke between the two girls. Ever since Jess had switched to slip on shoes, she would ask Emily this, even though she only had one pair.

"You do," Emily laughed, "You're good."

"You know, I'll miss some things," Jess said, "like feeling her move around. That really is a unique sensation, but I can't wait to see my feet again."

"Do you ever worry?" Emily asked.

Her serious tone chilled Jess's playful mood as she knew exactly what Emily was asking. Even though she prayed, the thought plagued her nightly. Sometimes just a passing thought, but sometimes an agonizing hour-long focus. Could she and Chad really give this girl a good life?

"I do," Jess nodded, "but Chad has been amazing. I know it won't be easy, but we will be okay. After all, we have God with us, and I know for sure we're going to love this girl."

The front door swung open, and Chad's dark head popped in. "Hey, you two ready yet? I'm starving. I've been thinking about brunch since I woke up."

"We're ready," Jess said as she waddled toward the door. "I just move slower these days."

"I know," he said, planting a kiss on Jess when she reached the doorway, "but you're still beautiful."

"Ah, come on, you two," Emily teased. "It's a good thing I haven't eaten yet."

"Your day will come," Jess said as she locked the door. "I hear Randall's been coming around to see you."

A rosy blush colored Emily's cheek before she could turn her head. Jess laughed. She was glad Emily had found someone and Jess knew Randall was a good guy.

Though the IHOP wasn't far, the trio loaded up in the SUV as the distance was too much for Jess to walk in her current condition. Just going up and down the stairs left her winded, and by the end of the day, she would have to prop her feet up to let them rest after walking all over campus.

"I'm so glad it's summer break," Jess said as she stretched the seatbelt across her belly. "I'm going to spend all day tomorrow just sitting on the couch."

"You can have one day," Chad said, "but remember the doctor said you should keep moving."

"Yeah, yeah," Jess said in a good-natured tone. "Just drive. I've been craving pancakes with blueberry syrup for a week now."

Chad smiled and pulled out of the parking lot.

~

"To a wonderful year," Chad said holding up his glass of orange juice as the trio finished their food.

"Cheers," the girls agreed and clinked glasses. Jess lifted the glass to her mouth for a sip and then froze. Her eyes widened.

"What is it?" Chad asked, his eyes wide with concern.

"It's time."

There was a moment of silence and then everyone spurred into action, speaking at the same time. "I'll get the check, I'll start the car, Are you okay?" Emily grabbed the keys from Chad and darted out the door.

Chad waved the waitress over and asked her for the bill. When the waitress returned, he didn't even look at the bill, just pulled two twenties out of his pocket and threw them in the black folder. Then he hurried to Jess's side of the table and held out his hand to help her up.

Emily had the SUV running as they reached the parking lot and Chad helped Jess into the front seat before climbing in the back. After buckling in, he pulled out his cell phone to text his family.

"What are you doing?" Chad asked as he noticed Jess retrieving her phone as well. "Aren't you in pain?"

She paused for a minute as if thinking. "Actually, no." Her eyes widened. "Is that a bad thing?"

"How would I know?" He threw his hands up in the air in a gesture of exasperation and then tugged one through his hair, creating an uneven part. "I've never had a baby."

A small smile tugged at Jess's lips. "Neither have I," she reminded him. "It's my first time too, so I have no idea what to expect."

"Don't look at me," Emily said from the driver's seat. "I'm still a virgin."

As Chad laughed, his nerves calmed a little. They were in this together, and everything would be okay.

~

*A*s the whooshing hospital doors parted at the trio's entrance, the nurse at the front desk looked up at them.

"Can I help you?" she asked.

"Yes, ma'am," Jess said. "I'm pretty sure my water broke."

"You're pretty sure?" The woman asked. "You mean you don't know?"

"Well, it's my first time in labor, so I'm not sure what to expect, but there was a lot of liquid."

"Al' right, we'll have the doctor

confirm," the nurse said. She turned to her computer and clicked several times on her mouse. "Let's get you checked in."

When the check-in was complete, an orderly appeared with a wheelchair and whisked Jess down the hallway to room 105. He helped her out of the chair and onto the hospital bed before exiting the room and leaving her alone, momentarily.

The door opened a minute later, and a dark-haired nurse entered the room holding a blue hospital gown. "Hi, I'm Nancy," she said. "We need you to get changed into this. Dr. Stevens will come check you. If your water has broken, we'll get you moved to a delivery room and your husband and friend can join you."

"Thank you," Jess said as she took the gown. As soon as Nancy exited the small room, Jess climbed down from the bed, removed her street clothes, and put the gown on. It was a cloth one at least with little white flowers, but it was still completely open in the back. Jess couldn't tie it herself, so the cool air sent shivers down her spine.

A knock sounded and a short woman with graying hair entered the room. "Hello, I'm Dr. Stevens," she said as she crossed to the antibacterial dispenser and rubbed some on her hands. "I hear you think your water broke."

"I'm fairly certain," Jess said, "but it is my first birth."

"Congratulations," Dr. Stevens said. "Okay, lay back and put your feet here in the stirrups."

Jess did, trying to ignore the cold that was creeping in through her socks. The doctor poked and prodded a bit, and Jess tried not to grimace. She hated this part, always had.

"Well, your water definitely broke,"

the doctor said. "You aren't feeling any contractions though?"

"I don't think so," Jess said. "I'm not feeling any pain."

"All right, we'll give it another few hours to see if labor kicks in. If not, we'll put you on a Pitocin drip. I don't want to let it go too long with your water broken."

Jess nodded though she had no idea what that meant. No one had ever mentioned Pitocin in the few birthing classes she had attended, and all the movies she had watched had the women screaming in labor shortly after their water broke.

The doctor exited, and Nancy returned to help Jess down the hall to the delivery room. Chad and Emily were already inside. Chad jumped up from the chair he had been sitting in as Jess entered.

"Calm down," Jess said. "No active labor yet."

Nancy helped her into the bed and then attached a belt-like device around her stomach. "This will monitor your contractions," Nancy said, "so don't take it off. It's on a long cord so you can stretch it into the bathroom. I'll leave my number on the board for you." She pointed to a small whiteboard on the wall. "Call if you need anything."

As Nancy exited, Chad crossed to the bedside and took Jess's hand. His hand was sweaty and warm. "You sure you're ready for this?" she asked.

"Not at all," he said, shaking his head, but a smile remained on his lips. "We'll figure it out though."

The next few hours flew by in a whirlwind. Chad's family arrived, bringing balloons and flowers. Jess's mother showed up moments later and introductions flowed around the room. Emily and Randall entered after that, having returned with clothes for Jess and the packed diaper bag that had been sitting by the front door of Chad and Jess's apartment in preparation for this day.

Then the doctor entered to check on Jess's progress again. Her eyes widened a little at the number of people in the room, but she politely asked them to stand back as she grabbed the white readout paper from the machine to the left of the bed. Her forehead wrinkled as she surveyed.

"Are you feeling any contractions yet?" Dr. Stevens asked, turning her dark eyes on Jess.

"I don't think so," Jess said. "I have some discomfort, but no pain. Would it be pain?"

The doctor nodded, almost absently, and then checked the belt around Jess's stomach again. "It looks like we'll have to give you Pitocin to speed up the labor," she said, and her fingers clicked across the keyboard of the computer.

Jess's pulse quickened at the words. "Can it wait? I'd like to have as natural a labor as possible."

"I can give you two more hours, but no longer. We don't want to risk infection."

Jess nodded. Two hours wasn't that long, but hopefully it would be long enough.

The doctor shuffled out of the room, and the tense silence descended again. Eyes shifted back and forth. No one seemed to know what to say. Jess readjusted her position in the bed, trying to get more comfortable, and the small move seemed to break the stillness.

Chad's father offered to pray for the delivery, for Jess, and for the future of the baby. Everyone circled around the bed and clasped hands.

~

Nancy entered a few hours later and put her hands on her hips. "I don't know how you all got in here, but we have a three-guest limit in the room during delivery. Some of you will need to go wait in the main waiting room until after the baby comes."

Everyone looked to the person nearest them. No one wanted to volunteer to leave, which left the decision up to Jess. She knew she wanted Emily in the room, and even though she felt closer to Chad's mother than to her own, the look in her mother's eyes said she would be disappointed if she couldn't stay. "Okay, Chad, Emily, and Mom can stay until the baby is born. Then the others can come back, right?"

Nancy nodded, and the others shuffled from the room.

"So, Chad, where are you from?" Jess's mother asked. Though they had met twice before, Jess's mother had been more focused on Jess those times and hadn't asked Chad many questions at all.

"California originally, but we moved to Texas when I was in High School because my dad got a job here."

"And what do you do?" It was odd to see her mother taking such an interest in a man in her life, but nice at the same time.

"Right now, I'm a TA for a psychology class, but eventually I hope to have my own counseling practice."

"Really?" Jess asked from the bed. He had never mentioned wanting to be a counselor.

"What else would I do with a

psychology degree?" he asked, a smile stretching across his face. "You pretty much either have to teach or be a counselor."

The nurse re-entered with a clear bag and hooked up the IV. "You should start feeling this soon; it might be a little cold. If you start feeling contractions and want the epidural, just hit the button, and I'll send the anesthesiologist in."

As the cold liquid entered her arm, Jess cringed. It wasn't exactly painful, but the feeling of ice mingling with blood wasn't comfortable either. An uncontrollable shiver ran over her body.

"Would you like an extra blanket?" the nurse asked.

Jess nodded as her teeth began to chatter slightly. The nurse ducked out of the room, returning a minute later with a warm blanket. Slowly the chills subsided, and Jess began to warm up again. With the heat came an intense pain in her abdomen. Her eyes widened, and she held her breath until the pain ceased. Had that been a contraction? The paper readout of the monitor next to her displayed a spike in the graph, confirming the hypothesis.

"Was that a contraction?" Emily asked.

Jess nodded, her jaw slowly unclenching. The pain had been bad, but not unbearable. As the afternoon wore on though, it became harder to tolerate. When she could stand it no longer, Jess punched the button on the call pad. The nurse popped in a few moments later, took one look at Jess's face, and left the room again promising to be right back.

When she re-entered, she had another new face with her. "This is Michael. He'll administer the epidural."

Relief flooded Jess at the words. She had wanted to be strong, but the pain had quickly become unbearable. Michael and Nancy helped her sit up and lean forward – not an easy task with a large belly.

Michael cautioned her to be still, but the contractions were even stronger when she leaned forward. Tears flooded Jess's eyes at the intensity of the pain. Chad hurried over, offering support and distraction until the needle was inserted in her back.

The pain dulled as they helped Jess lay back. A glorious numbness took over. The nurse checked the read out again before exiting the room with Michael.

"Better?" Chad asked.

Jess nodded. There was now just a dull throb, but none of the intense pain. The time seemed to pass ever more slowly. The nurse returned, checking the monitor read out again.

"Are you feeling any contractions?" she asked.

Jess shook her head. The pain was completely gone.

The nurse's brow furrowed, and she left the room, returning a moment later with the doctor. "Feeling no pain, Jess?" she asked.

"Nothing. Should I be?" A tiny inkling of fear stirred in her belly.

"I'm sure it's all fine. Let's take a look, shall we?" She motioned for the others to stand at the far end of the room, so she could perform the physical examination again. "Oh, there's the top of the head, so it looks like we're ready. I need you to push the next time you feel a contraction."

"But I'm not feeling any contractions," Jess said, fear mounting in her heart. "I don't feel anything."

"No worries," Dr. Stevens smiled, "I'll tell you when to push."

As Nancy took her place beside the

doctor, Chad hurried to the head of the bed and grabbed Jess's hand.

"Okay push," the doctor said.

Jess pushed like the nurse had told her, hoping she was doing it correctly.

"Okay, relax. And push again."

The process continued a few more minutes, and then the baby cried. Jess's heart seized with emotion. The nurse placed the baby on her chest for a minute as the doctor finished checking Jess. When the doctor was finished, Nancy took the baby to be weighed, measured, and checked. A few minutes later, Nancy returned with the baby bundled in a receiving blanket.

"Are you ready to hold her?"

Jess nodded and held out her arms. The tiny baby was perfect. Just a dusting of black fuzz covered her head. Jess's heart filled with love. She would move heaven and earth for this child, and as

Chad leaned in to look at the baby, Jess saw the same emotion in his eyes.

"She's so beautiful," he said, touching her head hesitantly.

"Yes, she is." Jess kissed her tiny angel on the forehead, then motioned her mother and Emily over. A smile broke out on her mother's face as she approached. Regret and love fought for prominent placement on her face.

When the doctor and nurse were finished with all the checks on the baby and Jess, they left the room, allowing the rest of the brood in the waiting room to join the group. Baby Kayleigh was passed back and forth, oohed and aahed over, rocked, and cuddled by everyone in the room.

At the end of visiting hours, the new nurse on shift came and asked everyone to leave. Chad and Jess were left alone in the room, which now seemed unnaturally quiet without the noise from everyone else.

Jess held the sleeping angel, stroking her hair while she slept, and poured her heart out to the little girl. "Darling daughter, we didn't do this right, but we promise to love you and do all that we can to give you the best life possible." Jess kissed the little button nose and looked up at Chad who smiled before kissing her forehead lightly.

Jess spent the night with Kayleigh curled in her arm. When the nurses would come in to check the vitals, they would always point out the bassinet. "You could get better sleep," they would say, but Jess shook her head. Sleep was not necessary tonight, but bonding with her daughter was.

Jess's eyes wandered to Chad's sleeping form on the couch. The love he had for his daughter had shone from his eyes every time he held her, and Jess knew that whatever might come, he would always do what was best for Kayleigh. He would never be like the abusive father figures that had been in Jess's past.

With a smile, Jess reflected on the past year and how different her life had turned out all because of a perky blonde and her God.

The End!

While this is the end of the Heartbeats series for now, keep reading for a sneak peek at my Star Lake series starting with When Love Returns!

AUTHOR'S NOTE

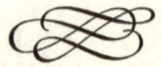

When I first wrote When Hearts Collide, Jess was Amanda's roommate, but then I decided Jess needed her own story and her chance at redemption. Thus, A Past Forgiven was born.

I really enjoy writing redemptive fiction because I know that people aren't perfect, but through God's love and refining, we all become better.

I hope you enjoyed this story. If you did, would you do me a favor? If you did, please leave a review. It really helps. It doesn't have to be long - just a few words to help other readers know what they're getting.

I'd love to hear from you, not only about this story, but about the characters or stories you'd like read in the future. I'm always looking for new ideas and if I use one of your characters or stories, I'll send you a free ebook and paperback of the book with a special dedication. Write to me at loranahoopes@gmail.com. And if you'd like to see what's coming next, be sure to stop by authorloranahoopes.com

I also have a weekly newsletter that contains many wonderful things like pictures of my adorable children, chances to win awesome prizes, new releases and sales I might be holding, great books from other authors, and anything else that strikes my fancy and that I think you would enjoy. I'll even send you the first chapter of my newest (maybe not even released yet) book if you'd like to sign up.

*E*ven better, I solemnly swear to only send out one newsletter a week (usually on Tuesday unless life gets in the way which with three kids it usually does). I will not spam you, sell your email address to solicitors or anyone else, or any of those other terrible things.

*T*urn the page for a sneak peek at a new series starting with **When Love Returns!**

NOT READY TO SAY GOODBYE YET?

*L*ove Jess and Chad? Well, you'll see Jess again for a minute in The Still Small Voice, but until then, why not journey to Star Lake and meet a whole new cast of characters?

When Love Returns

She loved him but couldn't tell him...

Presley knew she loved Brandon in high school, but when Morgan came into town and stole his heart, she knew she had to get away.

He wants a better life for his daughter...

Unfortunately he thinks that means

working all the time, but when his father falls, Brandon must return to Star Lake. He had no idea Presley had moved back.

When love returns....

Will Brandon realize the love he seeks is right in front of him?

Read on for a taste of When Love Returns....

WHEN LOVE RETURNS
PREVIEW

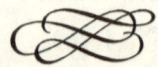

There it was. The one stoplight Brandon thought he'd never see again, still blinking its irregular red pattern that no one ever paid attention to. As most of the shops were centrally located, few people drove in town. Their cars were used for driving to neighboring cities when what they wanted wasn't available in town. There was no real need for the stop light, but the people had decided the town needed at least one stoplight to be called a proper town, and so it had been erected.

There had been a huge ceremony the day it was christened; the whole town had shown up. The mayor had been forced to stand on a ladder to cut the red ribbon as someone had placed it too high. Once he was up the ladder, another member of the city board handed him a giant pair of silver scissors. Then it became a balancing act as the mayor tried to open the giant scissors without losing his balance – that had been comical – and the town had watched in awe as the stoplight blinked, blinked, long pause, blinked, blinked.

The awe had faded quickly, and a squabble had broken out among the adults about the brand new broken light. The whole affair had been rather disappointing to a sixteen-year-old, who had been looking forward to getting his driver's license. That day was the nail in the coffin that solidified Brandon's idea of leaving the tiny backwards town and returning to normalcy.

Then he had met Presley, and his life changed.

"Are we there yet, Daddy?"

Brandon glanced in the rearview mirror at his daughter, Joy, strapped in her car seat. Her dark curls came from him, but her blue-grey eyes were her mother's. Joy was the one good thing that came out of this town.

"Almost, Bug."

She resumed her stare out the window as they continued down Main Street. The Diner still sat on the corner, probably still run by Max, the same uninspired owner who wore a ball cap and plaid flannel shirt to work every day. His choice of attire left a lot to be desired, but he was a good cook. To this day, Brandon was not sure he'd had a better burger.

Next to the diner was the small Post Office. Brandon had never spent much time there growing up, but he knew the man who worked there, Bert. An odd man to say the least – always trying out new ideas that never seemed to work. One year, he had tried raising chickens to supply eggs for the general store, but he had become attached to one of the chickens, naming her Stella and carrying her from place to place in a little bag like wealthy old women do with tiny dogs. The chicken had escaped the bag one day in the middle of The Diner and wreaked havoc, incensing Max. Stella disappeared after that, and Brandon was fairly certain she ended up on Max's menu, but he could never prove it.

The general store appeared next. It carried groceries and a small selection of clothing and household goods. Brandon had been shocked by the meager selection when he first arrived, but the town wore on him and had a way of making him forget the outside world moving on around it. By the time he graduated high school, Brandon had been accustomed to the small offerings until he arrived in Dallas and felt like a total hick, at least three years behind the times.

"Daddy, look, cupcakes. Can we get one?"

Twisting in the black leather seat, Brandon followed her finger pointing out the opposite window. There had been no cupcake shop four years ago, but there was indeed a shop there now, where the laundromat had been, sporting a colorful cupcake sign and logo on the window. Sweet Treats. Not a highly original name, but neither were most of the stores in town.

"We'll come back by later." Brandon was curious about the owner. Who would choose to put up a new shop in this sleepy little town?

Her bottom lip turned out in an adorable pout, but she didn't continue to fight him. For her, this trip was like a vacation to a new and unusual place. The two rarely ventured from Dallas, mainly because Brandon's work kept him too busy for vacations. For him, it was a return to a past he had hoped to forget. Too much pain and too much sadness resided in this little town.

Brandon made a right down Cooper Street, the road that led to his parent's house. Though it had been years since he had been back, he could drive the route blindfolded, partly because it was a simple route, and partly because he walked it so many times as a teenager.

The two-story yellow house looked

exactly as he remembered it, though the paint was chipping in a few more places and faded in others. The gravel of the driveway crunched under the tires as he pulled in. Brandon parked the car and took a deep breath.

"Let me out Daddy," Joy called from the back seat.

Sighing, he opened his door and then reached in to unbuckle her. Though five, she was still too small to qualify for a booster seat, and Brandon felt safer having her in the bigger car seat anyway. No one ever told him that when he became a parent, he would have crazy nightmares about all the ways he could lose his daughter. The car accident was always the worst.

Joy scurried out of the car, her faded pink bunny clutched in one petite hand. On the day she was born, Brandon's mother had given her a soft pink cuddle bunny. Joy latched onto it, sleeping with it every night. When she began crawling, she would often pick up the bunny in her mouth, dragging it across the floors. Even after she began walking, the bunny would go outside with her to play in the dirt or be flung around the room. The bunny had seen better days, but she refused to part with it for any longer than an occasional trip in the washing machine, and of course, no one sold this bunny any longer. Brandon had scoured the internet one day looking for a replacement, but come up empty. He dreaded the day it fell apart, and he couldn't replace it.

As Joy scrambled up the wooden porch, Brandon popped the trunk and grabbed the two suitcases he packed the night before. His hope was that they'd only be here a week, but he had no guarantee and therefore packed for at least two.

Joy was banging on the door when Brandon reached her side. She hadn't been around his parents much, as Brandon had moved to Dallas shortly after Joy's first birthday, but they had visited a few times. Joy always clung to them when they did as if she knew the time wouldn't be for very long. Now, she had created this idea in her head of what they would be like while she was here and regaled Brandon with it the last few days. He hoped she wouldn't be disappointed, but was afraid she might. His mother probably wouldn't be able to spend much time with her as she would be taking care of his father, at least when he got released from the hospital.

Brandon's mother opened the door and broke into a smile. She looked older than he remembered. More lines crossed her face and more grey streaks colored her hair, but her eyes still twinkled the way they always had.

"Joy." She bent down with her arms out.

"Nana." Joy ran into her arms, squeezing the woman tightly about the neck. "You smell like cookies."

A smile played across Brandon's lips. His mother always smelled of vanilla and sugar, and while she had often had a plate of cookies waiting for him when he arrived home from school, she hadn't every day, and he wondered how she still smelled of cookies on those days.

"That's because I have some in the kitchen." She tapped the end of Joy's nose, earning a giggle. "Now, come in, and let's get you settled."

"Then can we have cookies?" Joy bounced up and down, sending the lights in her pink sneakers into overdrive. His mother nodded, smiling at her enthusiasm.

Brandon pulled the two suitcases into the homey entrance and shut the door behind him.

The house hadn't changed a bit. A wooden coatrack still sat just to the right of the front door, holding his father's derby cap and a few coats, and the sign, announcing "As for me and my house, we will serve the Lord," still hung prominently on the wall. Brandon shed his coat, adding it to the rack and then removed Joy's as well.

"Let me show you to your room." His mother grabbed Joy's free hand and led her down the beige carpeted hallway. Pictures of Brandon and his sister, Anna, lined the walls. His mother never let an opportunity to take a picture go by, and Brandon was almost certain she bought every school picture they ever had so she could display them all on the walls. He had tried to remove one once and replace it with something else, but she noticed right away and forced him to rehang the picture.

His mother opened the door to the guest room. She had obviously added some decorations for a younger child to enjoy. The daybed had been covered with a flowery pink and purple bedspread, and a blond doll sat propped on top. An old dollhouse was near the dresser along with a faded toy box filled with toys.

"This is all for me?" Joy's eyes were wide as she looked up at Brandon's mother.

The lines around his mother's eyes grew more visible as she smiled. "Yep, all for you. A girl needs proper toys."

"Especially in this town," he said under his breath. Not quietly enough though as his mother shot a look full of daggers his direction. How quickly she could change from sugar to fire. Brandon held his hand up in silent apology.

"Where is Daddy staying?"

"Right across the hall." His mother opened the door to Brandon's old room which looked very much like it had in high school. His football awards still lined the shelf, though a fine layer of dust coated them now, and the tattered posters of his favorite bands covered the walls.

"Didn't feel like updating this one?" he asked.

His mother shrugged. "Maybe I would have if you came around more often."

Brandon wanted to reply, but he didn't want to start a fight, so he bit his tongue and carried the suitcase inside. After dropping off Joy's suitcase as well, they followed his mother back towards the open living room and into the country-themed kitchen. Brandon hated the flowered wallpaper trim that circled the kitchen, but his mother hung it herself and had always loved it.

A plate of chocolate chip cookies sat in the middle of the scratched kitchen table. The usual wild flower display had been pushed to the side. Joy turned eager eyes on Brandon, the unasked question evident.

"You may have one." He held up a finger. "I don't want you to spoil your dinner."

She climbed up in a chair and snatched a cookie off the top of the pile, shoving most of it in her mouth.

Brandon shook his head. "You could chew more slowly."

Her ravenous munching changed to a thoughtful chewing, and he joined her at the table, plucking a cookie for himself off the pile.

"How is Dad?" Brandon asked before taking a bite. His father was the whole reason he was here. He was in the hospital after falling off a ladder and fracturing his skull. Though Brandon's mother claimed he hadn't needed to come, he couldn't very well stay in Dallas if there was a chance this was life threatening, and brain bleeds often were.

Plus, he figured his mother might need some help with his father when he got released. He would probably not be as active as he was before the accident. However, Brandon was in the middle of a big presentation, one that could set him up for life with an even bigger company, so he had left strict instructions with his assistant to keep him in the loop.

A flicker of doubt erased his mother's twinkling eyes for a moment before she recovered. "He is doing better today. The nurses say he only had a few instances of confusion yesterday, but they want to run another CT tomorrow."

"Any idea on when he'll be released?" Brandon took a bite of the cookie, enjoying the warm chocolate goodness. He had missed his mom's cooking.

"Probably another few days, but it depends on what the scan shows. He has a pretty big brain bleed."

"Your brain can bleed?" Joy's head popped up, her eyes as wide as saucers.

His mother shot an apologetic look and without saying it, the two agreed to finish the discussion later when little ears were not present.

"Don't worry." Brandon patted her arm. "The brain is amazing and can heal itself. When does Anna get in?" Anna, his younger sister, was away at college studying to become a nurse.

"She has finals this week, so she's

coming as soon as she finishes the last one. Oh, and guess who else is back in town?"

Brandon raised an eyebrow at her; he had never been a fan of the guessing game.

"Presley Hays."

Presley Hays. The name knocked the wind out of him like a sucker punch. He hadn't thought of her in years. In high school, Presley had been his best friend — the one person who had made this town bearable — but for some reason they had grown apart when Morgan entered the picture, and then one day Presley had come over to tell him she was going to France to attend Le Cordon Bleu.

"The cupcake shop?" Brandon said the words for himself, but his mother smiled and nodded.

"Who's Presley?" Joy looked from Brandon to his mother.

"Just an old friend," Brandon said. *Just an old friend.*

Click to continue reading When Love Returns.

Or get all 3 books in the Star Lake series for a 20% savings.

A FREE STORY FOR YOU

~

*E*njoyed this story? Not ready to quit reading yet? If you sign up for my newsletter, you will receive The Billionaire's Impromptu Bet right away as my thank you gift for choosing to hang out with me.

The Billionaire's Impromptu Bet

A SWAT officer. A bored billionaire heiress. A bet that could change everything....

Read on for a taste of The Billionaire's Impromptu Bet....

THE BILLIONAIRE'S IMPROMPTU BET PREVIEW

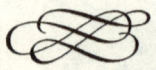

*B*rie Carter fell back spread eagle on her queen-sized canopy bed sending her blond hair fanning out behind her. With a large sigh, she uttered, "I'm bored."

"How can you be bored? You have like millions of dollars." Her friend, Ariel, plopped down in a seated position on the bed beside her and flicked her raven hair off her shoulder. "You want to go shopping? I hear Tiffany's is having a special right now."

Brie rolled her eyes. Shopping? Where was the excitement in that? With her three platinum cards, she could go shopping whenever she wanted. "No, I'm bored with shopping too. I have everything. I want to do something exciting. Something we don't normally do."

Brie enjoyed being rich. She loved the unlimited credit cards at her disposal, the constant apparel of new clothes, and of course the penthouse apartment her father paid for, but lately, she longed for something more fulfilling.

Ariel's hazel eyes widened. "I know. There's a new bar down on Franklin Street. Why don't we go play a little game?"

Brie sat up, intrigued at the secrecy and the twinkle in Ariel's eyes. "What kind of game?"

"A betting game. You let me pick out

any man in the place. Then you try to get him to propose to you."

Brie wrinkled her nose. "But I don't want to get married." She loved her freedom and didn't want to share her penthouse with anyone, especially some man.

"You don't marry him, silly. You just get him to propose."

Brie bit her lip as she thought. It had been awhile since her last relationship and having a man dote on her for a month might be interesting, but.... "I don't know. It doesn't seem very nice."

"How about I sweeten the pot? If you win, I'll set you up on a date with my brother."

Brie cocked her head. Was she serious? The only thing Brie couldn't seem to buy in the world was the affection of Ariel's very handsome, very wealthy, brother. He was a movie star, just the kind of person Brie could consider marrying in the future. She'd had a crush on him as long as she and Ariel had been friends, but he'd always seen her as just that, his little sister's friend. "I thought you didn't want me dating your brother."

"I don't." Ariel shrugged. "But he's between girlfriends right now, and I know you've wanted it for ages. If you win this bet, I'll set you up. I can't guarantee any more than one date though. The rest will be up to you."

Brie wasn't worried about that. Charm she possessed in abundance. She simply needed some alone time with him, and she was certain she'd be able to convince him they were meant to be together. "All right. You've got a deal."

Ariel smiled. "Perfect. Let's get you changed then and see who the lucky man will be.

A tiny tug pulled on Brie's heart that

this still wasn't right, but she dismissed it. This was simply a means to an end, and he'd never have to know.

~

*J*esse Calhoun relaxed as the rhythmic thudding of the speed bag reached his ears. Though he loved his job, it was stressful being the SWAT sniper. He hated having to take human lives and today had been especially rough. The team had been called out to a drug bust, and Jesse was forced to return fire at three hostiles. He didn't care that they fired at his team and himself first. Taking a life was always hard, and every one of them haunted his dreams.

"You gonna bust that one too?" His co-worker Brendan appeared by his side. Brendan was the opposite of Jesse in nearly every way. Where Jesse's hair was a dark copper, Brendan's was nearly black. Jesse sported paler skin and a dusting of freckles across his nose, but Brendan's skin was naturally dark and freckle free.

Jesse flashed a crooked grin, but kept his eyes on the small, swinging black bag. The speed bag was his way to release, but a few times he had started hitting while still too keyed up and he had ruptured the bag. Okay, five times, but who was counting really? Besides, it was a better way to calm his nerves than other things he could choose. Drinking, fights, gambling, women.

"Nah, I think this one will last a little longer." His shoulders began to burn, and he gave the bag another few punches for good measure before dropping his arms and letting it swing to a stop. "See? It lives to be hit at least another day." Every once in a while, Jesse missed training the way he used to. Before he joined the force, he had been an amateur boxer, on his way to being a pro, but a shoulder injury had delayed his training and forced him to consider something else. It had eventually healed, but by then he had lost his edge.

"Hey, why don't you come drink with us?" Brendan clapped a hand on Jesse's shoulder as they headed into the locker room.

"You know I don't drink." Jesse often felt like the outsider of the team. While half of the six-man team was married, the other half found solace in empty bottles and meaningless relationships. Jesse understood that - their job was such that they never knew if they would come home night after night - but he still couldn't partake.

Brendan opened his locker and pulled out a clean shirt. He peeled off his current one and added deodorant before tugging on the new one. "You don't have to drink. Look, I won't drink either. Just come and hang out with us. You have no one waiting for you at home."

That wasn't entirely true. Jesse had Bugsy, his Boston Terrier, but he understood Brendan's point. Most days, Jesse went home, fed Bugsy, made dinner, and fell asleep watching TV on the couch. It wasn't much of a life. "All right, I'll go, but I'm not drinking."

Brendan's lips pulled back to reveal his perfectly white teeth. He bragged about them, but Jesse knew they were veneers. "That's the spirit. Hurry up and change. We don't want to leave the rest of the team waiting."

"Is everyone coming?" Jesse pulled out his shower necessities. Brendan might feel comfortable going out with just a new application of deodorant, but Jesse needed to wash more than just dirt and sweat off. He needed to wash the sound of the bullets and the sight of lifeless bodies from his mind.

"Yeah, Pat's wife is pregnant again and demanding some crazy food concoctions. Pat agreed to pick them up if she let him have an hour. Cam and Jared's wives are having a girls' night, so the whole gang can be together. It will be nice to hang out when we aren't worried about being shot at."

"Fine. Give me ten minutes. Unlike you, I like to clean up before I go out."

Brendan smirked. "I've never had any complaints. Besides, do you know how long it takes me to get my hair like this?"

Jesse shook his head as he walked into the shower, but he knew it was true. Brendan had rugged good looks and muscles to match. He rarely had a hard time finding a woman. Jesse on the other hand hadn't dated anyone in the last few months. It wasn't that he hadn't been looking, but he was quieter than his teammates. And he wasn't looking for right now. He was looking for forever. He just hadn't found it yet.

Click here to continue reading The Billionaire's Impromptu Bet.

DISCUSSION QUESTIONS

1. What did you like best about this book?

2. What did you like least about this book?

3. What other books does this remind you of?

4. Share a favorite quote from the book. Why did this stand out to you?

5. Would you read another book by this author? Why or why not?

6. What feelings did this book invoke in you?

7. If you got the chance to ask the author of this book one question, what would it be?

8. What do you think of the book's title? How does it relate to the book's contents? What other title might you choose?

9. What do you think of the book's cover? How well does it convey what the book is about? If the book has been published with different covers, which one did you like the best?

THE STORY DOESN'T END!

You've met a few people and fallen in love….

I bet you're wondering how you can meet everyone else.

Star Lake Series:

When Love Returns: The first in the Star Lake series. Presley Hays and Brandon Scott were best friends in High School until Morgan entered their town and stole Brandon's heart. Devastated, Presley takes a scholarship to Le Cordon

Bleu, but five years later, she is back in Star Lake after a tough breakup. Brandon thought he'd never return to Star Lake after Morgan left him and his daughter Joy, but when his father needs help, he returns home and finds more than he bargained for. Can Presley and Brandon forget past hurts or will their stubborn natures keep them apart forever?

Once Upon a Star: The second book in the Star Lake series. Audrey left Star Lake to pursue acting, but after an unplanned pregnancy her jobs and her money dwindled, leaving her no option except to return home and start over. Blake was the quintessential nerd in high school and was never able to tell Audrey how he felt. Now that he's gained confidence and some muscle, will he finally be able to reveal his feelings? Once Upon a Star will take you back to Christmas in Star Lake. Revisit your favorite characters and meet a few ones in this sweet Christmas read.

Love Conquers All: Lanie Perkins Hall never imagined being divorced at thirty. Nor did she imagine falling for an old friend, but when she runs into Azarius Jacobson, she can't deny the attraction. As they begin to spend more time together, Lanie struggles with the fact Azarius keeps his past a secret. What is he hiding? And will she ever be able to get him to open up? Azarius Jacobson has loved Lanie Perkins Hall from the moment he saw her, but issues from his past have left him guarded. Now that he has another chance with her, will he find the courage to share his life with her? Or will his emotional walls create a barrier that will leave him alone once more? Find out in this heartfelt, emotional third book (stand alone) in the Star Lake series.

The Heartbeats Series:

Where It All Began: Sandra Baker thought her life was on the right track until she ended up pregnant. Her boyfriend, not wanting the baby, pushes her to have an abortion. After the procedure, Sandra's life falls apart, and she turns to alcohol. Her relationship ends, and she struggles to find meaning in her life. When she meets Henry Dobbs, a strong Christian man, she begins to wonder if God would accept her. Will she tell Henry her darkest secret? And will she ever be able to forgive herself and find healing? Find out in this emotional love story.

The Power of Prayer: Callie Green thought she had her whole life planned out until her fiance left her at the altar. When her carefully laid plans crumble, she begins to make mistakes at work and engage in uncharacteristic activities. After a mistake nearly costs her her job, she cashes in her honeymoon tickets for some time away. There she meets JD, a charming Christian man who, even though she is not a believer, captures her interest. Before their relationship can deepen, Callie's ex-fiance shows back up in her life and she is forced to choose between Daniel and JD. Who will she choose and how will her choice affect the rest of her life? Find out in this touching novel.

When Hearts Collide: Amanda Adams has always been a Christian, but she's a novice at relationships. When she meets Caleb, her emotions get the best of her and she ignores the sign that something is amiss. Will she find out before it's too late? Jared Masterson is still healing from his girlfriend's strange rejection and disappearance when he meets Amanda. She captivates his heart, but can he save her from making the biggest mistake of her life? A must read for mothers and daughters. Though part of the series and the first of the college spin off series, it is a stand alone book and can be read separately.

A Past Forgiven: Jess Peterson has lived a life of abuse and lost her self worth, but when she is paired with a Christian roommate, she begins to wonder if there is a loving father looking down on her. Her decisions lead her one way, but when she ends up pregnant, she must make some major changes. Chad Michelson is healing from his own past and uses meaningless relationships to hide his pain, but when Jess becomes pregnant, he begins to wonder about the meaning of life. Can he step up and be there for Jess and the baby?

Sweet Billionaires Series:
The Billionaire's Secret: Maxwell

Banks was the ultimate player until he found himself caring for a daughter he didn't know he had. Can he change to become the role model she needs? Alyssa Miller hasn't had the best luck with past relationships, so why is she falling for the one man who is sure to break her heart? Though nearly complete opposites, feelings develop, but can Max really change his philandering ways? Or will one mistake seal his fate forever?

A Brush with a Billionaire: Brent just wanted to finish his novel in peace, but when his car breaks down in Sweet Grove, he is forced to deal with a female mechanic and try to get along. Sam thought she had given up on city boys, but when Brent shows up in her shop, she finds herself fighting attraction. Will their stubborn natures keep them apart or can a small town festival bring them together?

The Billionaire's Christmas

Miracle: Drew Devonshire is captivated by the woman he meets at a masquerade ball, but who is she? Gwen Rodgers is a teacher, but when she pretends to be her friend and meets Drew at a masquerade ball, her world gets thrown upside down.

The Billionaire's Cowboy Groom: Carrie Bliss finally found the man she wants to marry but there's just one little problem. She's technically still married. Cal Roper hasn't seen her in years but his heart still belongs to his wife. When she returns to town requesting a divorce, can he convince her they belong together?

The Cowboy Billionaire: Coming Soon!

The Lawkeeper Series:

Lawfully Matched: Kate Whidby doesn't want to impose on her newly married brother after their parents die, so she accepts a mail order bride offer in the paper. Little does she know the man she intends to marry has a dark past, sending her fleeing into a neighboring town and into Jesse Jenning's life. Jesse never wanted to be in law enforcement, but after a band of robbers kills his fiancee, he dons the badge and swears revenge. Will he find his fiancee's killer? And when Kate flies into his life, will he be able to put his painful past behind him in order to love again?

Lawfully Justified: William Cook turns to bounty hunting after losing his wife. When he suffers a life-threatening injury, he is forced to stay in town with an intriguing woman. Emma Stewart has moved back in with her widowed father, the town doctor, but she still longs for a family of her own, so no one is more surprised than she is when she starts to develop feeling for the bounty hunter, who hides his heart of gold behind a rugged exterior. Can Emma offer William a reason to stay? Can William find a way to heal from his broken past to start a future with Emma? Or will a haunting secret take away all the possibilities of this budding romance?

The Scarlet Wedding: William and Emma are planning their wedding, but an outbreak and a return from his past force them to change their plans. Is a happily ever after still in their future?

Lawfully Redeemed: Dani Higgins is a K9 cop looking to make a name for herself, but she finds herself at the mercy of a stranger after an accident. Calvin Phillips just wanted to help his brother, but somehow he ended up in the middle of a police investigation and caring for the woman trying to bring his brother in.

The Still Small Voice Series:
The Still Small Voice: Jordan

Wright was searching for something after she gave her son up for adoption. What she found was God, and she began receiving visions. But can she trust Him when he asks her to do something big? Kat Jameson had long been a lukewarm Christian, but when her friend dies and she begins seeing lights, she thinks she is going crazy. Then she meets someone with a message for her. Will she be able to give up control and do what is asked of her?

A Spark in the Darkness coming soon!

Blushing Brides Series:

The Cowboy's Reality Bride: Tyler Hall just wanted to find love, but the women he dated wanted more than his small-town life provided. He gets more than he bargained for when he ends up on a reality dating show and falls for a woman who is not a contestant. Laney Swann has been running from her past for years, but it takes meeting a man on a reality dating show to make her see there's no need to run.

The Reality Bride's Baby: Laney wants nothing more than a baby, but when she starts feeling dizzy is it pregnancy or something more serious?

The Producer's Unlikely Bride: Justin Miller had given up on love, but when his image needs help, he finds himself needing the aid of a stranger who just happens to be a romance writer. Ava McDermott is waiting for the perfect love, but after agreeing to a fake relationship with Justin, she finds herself falling for real.

Ava's Blessing in Disguise: Five years after marriage, Ava faces a mysterious illness that threatens to ruin her career. Will she find out what it is?

The Soldier's Steadfast Bride: coming soon

The Men of Fire Beach

Fire Games: Cassidy returns home from Who Wants to Marry a Cowboy to find obsessive letters from a fan. The cop assigned to help her wants to get back to his case, but what she sees at a fire may just be the key he's looking for.

Lost Memories and New Beginnings: coming soon

Stand Alones:

Love Renewed: This books is part of the multi author second chance series. When fate reunites high school sweethearts separated by life's choices, can they find a second chance at love at a snowy lodge amid a little mystery?

Her children's early reader chapter book series:

The Wishing Stone #1: Dangerous Dinosaur

The Wishing Stone #2: Dragon Dilemma

The Wishing Stone #3: Mesmerizing Mermaids

The Wishing Stone #4: Pyramid Puzzle

The Wishing Stone Inspirations 1: Mary's Miracle

To see a list of all her books

authorloranahoopes.com
loranahoopes@gmail.com

ABOUT THE AUTHOR

Lorana Hoopes is an inspirational author originally from Texas but now living in the PNW with her husband and three children. When not writing, she can be seen kickboxing at the gym, singing, or acting on stage. One day, she hopes to retire from teaching and write full time.